Mavis backed away from me coyly when I took her up to the hotel room. I guess a girl likes a little sweet romance. She said plaintively, "Don't I even get asked?"

I didn't answer. I didn't have time for sweet romance. I wanted to teach her in a hurry who was going to be boss of our little arrangement. And what better way is there?

I pulled her to me suddenly and kissed her. In a moment, her arms slid up and her mouth became warm and eager under mine. I picked her up and carried her to the couch.

She learned fast. . . .

KISS AND KILL

Richard Deming

WILDSIDE PRESS

CHAPTER I

I suppose that in any profession you grow with experience. I know that I did. When I think of my crude planning in the early years, and the chances I took, it makes my hair curl. Time and again I blundered past disaster by pure luck.

But you learn as you go along. Nobody's luck holds forever, and in my business you're allowed only one bad break. Long ago I decided the only way to avoid that eventual bad break was to eliminate chance from my planning entirely. I've never taken a chance since.

When Mavis was in a teasing mood, she used to call me "the careful man."

I'm careful, all right. You have to be careful to get away with an average of three murders a year.

We sort of drifted into the business of murder. In the beginning neither Mavis nor I had any plans more serious than working bunco dodges. Maybe if we'd never met, neither of us would ever have turned to murder. But we did meet, and as a team we could hardly avoid moving into the big time. We complemented each other too beautifully to miss.

When I met Mavis six years ago, she was nearly as naïve as the typical mark.

We met at the Beverly-Wilshire, where we were both registered at the time. I was working on a well-to-do widow who was staying there. Mavis, she later told me, was merely looking for a prospect and had picked the Beverly-Wilshire as a likely place to find one.

My plans for the widow had just struck a snag. I was going to need a feminine partner to work the score, and I was sitting alone at the hotel bar mentally sorting over the women I knew in the profession. My mark, Mrs. Cora Hollingsworth, had flown up to Las Vegas for the day.

The trouble was that all the con-women I knew were used to posing as rich, sophisticated women of the world. And for this play, I needed someone to act the part of an ordinary working girl, youthful and unworldly. I doubted that any of them could swing it.

A young woman came into the bar, glanced around, and took a stool two places from mine. In a musical but rather affected voice, she said to the bartender, "A Tom Collins, please."

Giving her a cursory glance, I saw a slim, black-haired girl of about twenty-five, with a firm, well-formed body and disturbing green eyes. By conventional standards of beauty, her face was too thin, and her small white teeth were faintly irregular. Yet there was a sensual, entirely feminine quality about her which automatically quickened my pulse. Perhaps it was the ripe fullness of her lips, or merely her sultry expression. Whatever it was, it made me give her a second look.

She wore a plain knitted dress which at first glance looked expensive. But I was practiced in judging women's clothes, and decided it was only the attractive lines of the body beneath the dress that gave that impression. A duplicate could be bought in any department store for under thirty dollars. Her pumps and matching bag, also expensive-looking at first glance, were simulated

6

alligator. To top it off, she wore a wristwatch which glittered with fake diamonds and a ring set with a green stone which would have been worth several thousand dollars if it had been an emerald instead of tinted glass.

Her clothes, her affected tone in ordering her drink, and the rather theatrical condescension with which she laid a twenty-dollar bill on the bar tabbed her as a woman of limited means attempting to act as though she had money. It never occurred to me that she might be a fellow member of the profession, though. I pegged her as a working girl on vacation enjoying the harmless fantasy of being her favorite movie actress for a short time.

Exactly the type of girl I needed to work my score, I thought ruefully.

She covertly examined me at the same time I was looking her over. I seemed to make more of an impression on her than she did on me. Which wasn't surprising. Even in those days, I did know how to put on a front. My suit had cost a hundred and fifty dollars and my shoes were hand-tooled leather. Everything I wore was conservative but expensive. I looked like a young, successful executive.

The girl waited until the bartender was at the far end of the bar, then produced a cigarette and called to him in the same affected voice, "May I have a light, please?"

Her eyes flicked sidewise at me as she spoke. She was waiting for me to save the barkeep the trouble of walking the length of the bar by offering a light myself. Amused, I produced my lighter and held flame to her cigarette. The bartender, halfway to her, dropped a packet of matches back into the pocket of his white coat.

"Thank you," she said primly. "I left my gold lighter in my room."

The adjective "gold" amused me. She was as refreshingly naïve as a small girl playing princess. If I hadn't been in the process of working a dodge, I would have played along just for kicks. But I had too much on my mind to let myself get sidetracked by a flirtation. Finishing my drink, I gave her an impersonal smile and walked away.

At the door I looked back to see her crook her finger at the bartender. When the man came to her, she leaned forward to speak to him in a low tone. He glanced toward me, then quickly averted his eyes again when he saw me standing in the doorway watching. I continued on out, amused to know that the woman was inquiring who I was.

She would probably be impressed by what the bartender told her, I imagined. The hotel employees thought I was a vacationing executive of a New York importing firm which had branch offices all over the world.

I paused in the lobby, considering where I could go for some quiet, uninterrupted thinking. It was a sunny afternoon in late May, and the thought of spending it in my room wasn't very attractive.

I thought of the hotel swimming pool. The outside temperature was only about seventy, warm enough to be comfortable lying in the sun, yet cool enough to assure that the pool would be relatively deserted. Deciding I could think as well lying in the sun on my back as I could in my room, I walked out to the pool and rented a pair of trunks.

When I came from the dressing room, I brought a towel, a package of cigarettes and my lighter with me.

I laid them at the front edge of the pool, on the opposite side of the diving board from where the lifeguard was seated in a canvas chair, and dived in.

Except for the lifeguard and a young couple lying in the sun at the far edge of the pool, I had the place to myself. I did a few fancy dives, then stretched out on the concrete with my head on the towel to absorb some sun and think. I closed my eyes against the brightness of the sun.

A shadow touched my face, making me open my eyes. The girl I had seen in the bar, now wearing the briefest of blue bathing suits, stood over me. She must have gone up to her room to change, for it obviously wasn't a rented suit. Apparently she had followed me from the bar into the lobby and had seen me head for the pool. She was persistent when she wanted to meet a man, I thought sourly.

She carried a towel and a bathing cap in one hand, a package of cigarettes in the other. "Could I trouble you for another light?" she asked. "I forgot my lighter again."

This time I wasn't amused, because I had wanted to be alone. Sitting up, I asked dryly, "The gold one?"

"Why, yes," she said. "I only have one."

I flicked my lighter and she stooped to get the flame. Then she dropped to the edge of the pool about two feet away from me and dangled her feet in the water.

"Thank you," she said.

"Sure," I told her a little shortly. I fished a cigarette from my pack and lighted one of my own.

"I was watching you dive," she said. "You're quite expert, aren't you?"

"Run-of-the-mill. I was a summer lifeguard as a kid."

"Oh?" she said in an interested tone. "That accounts

9

for all those muscles. I've heard swimming is the best all-around exercise there is."

She was beginning to amuse me again. The asking-for-a-light technique was about the corniest approach in the book. Now she was going into the my-what-a-big-strong-man-you-are act.

"You have nice muscles yourself," I said.

She gave me a quick glance, blushed when she saw I was pointedly staring at her full bosom. For a flustered moment she didn't know what to say. I didn't help her any. I was interested to see how she handled wolf wise-cracks.

She simply ignored the remark. She asked, "Do you stay here?"

"Uh-huh," I said.

"So do I. I just checked in. I'm Mavis Train." She looked at me expectantly.

"Sam Carter," I said. "What's your room number?"

She looked a little startled. "What? Why, 713. Why?"

"I collect them," I said.

"Collect what?"

"Pretty girl's room numbers. Then when I get drunk and feel lecherous in the middle of the night, I go pound on their doors."

She stared at me, not sure whether I was making a joke or was really a screwball.

I said, "I'm just warning you. Didn't your mother ever tell you it's dangerous to speak to strange men?"

She decided I was teasing her. "I'm not that young," she told me. "I'm twenty-five."

"From where?" I asked.

"What? Oh, you mean my home. Long Island."

I nodded. "Your father has a big estate there?"

10

"Why, yes. How did you know?"

"Just a guess. What are you doing so far from home?"

She hesitated, then said with rehearsed reluctance, "I ran away from a wedding."

"Oh? Whose?"

"My own, silly. My father wanted me to marry this old man. Well, not old exactly. He's about forty-five. He's a business associate of daddy's."

The words had a familiar ring. They were the prelude to one of the oldest female bunco games there is. Old, but pretty effective when a real artist pulls it. But Mavis was no artist. Her idea of how heiresses acted was derived from seeing movies. Up to now I had assumed she was merely play-acting for the thrill of it. Now I realized with a shock that she was trying to work a bunco game and had picked me as her mark.

For a few moments I was too flabbergasted to speak. A little offended too. I regarded myself as an accomplished pro, and it wasn't very flattering to be taken for a sucker. Then the humor of the situation struck me.

"Daddy insists on the marriage, huh?" I said with a wide grin. "If you go home and behave, all will be forgiven. If you don't, he'll cut you off without a cent. Already you're running low on cash, and are becoming a little desperate. You've about decided to give in."

She examined me doubtfully. I was going too fast. That part of the story wasn't supposed to come out for several days yet, when I had become fond enough of her to object to her throwing her life away on a man twenty years older than she was.

"Don't go back home and marry him," I advised. "Something will come up. Maybe some kind man will

11

stake you until you can get a job and make it on your own."

She frowned and looked a little confused.

"How much do you need?" I asked.

She stared at me for a long time. Then she said accusingly, "You're making fun of me."

"Me?" I said. "Make fun of a damsel in distress? You wound me. Your story tugs at my heart. I'd open my purse wide, except for one thing."

She ground out her cigarette on the concrete and tossed it aside. Rising, she looked down at me disdainfully. "I don't think I like you, Mr. Carter."

"Don't you want to know what the one thing is?" I asked.

"No." Turning her back, she started to walk away.

"It's that there's very little in my purse," I said softly. "I'm in the bunco racket too."

She stopped and slowly turned around. Her eyes were wide as they stared down at me.

"Sit down again," I invited. "I've been looking for a girl like you. Maybe we can get together in a different way than you intended."

CHAPTER II

AFTER SILENTLY eyeing me for some time, she returned and gracefully sank to a position facing me. She looked wary.

"This your first attempt to score?" I asked.

After thinking this over, she said, "I don't know what you mean."

"Then it's your first attempt," I told her. "What gave you the idea of pulling the runaway heiress gag?"

She continued to study me. Finally she asked, "Are you really a confidence man?"

"Uh-huh."

"A good one?"

"Among the best," I said modestly. "You made a fine choice for your first mark. I spotted you for a phony the minute you walked in the bar."

She frowned. "How?"

"You ever actually know an heiress?" I countered.

She reluctantly shook her head.

"You overdid it. I didn't know it was a bunco pitch, of course. I just thought you were putting up a front for kicks. Like a little girl playing dress-up in her mother's clothes. I didn't realize you were trying to work a dodge until a few moments ago. But your front was so obvious, it was funny."

"You aren't very good for my ego," she said.

"I'm good for your welfare," I told her dryly. "With your technique, you were headed straight for jail."

She flushed a little. "Why are you telling me this?"

I looked her up and down. "With a little training, your technique might improve. You speak decent English. You're young and good-looking. With the proper clothes and a lot of polish, you *could* pass as an heiress."

"You mean you'd like to train me?" she asked eagerly.

"Maybe. Interested?"

"Oh, yes," she said enthusiastically. "I never thought I'd be lucky enough to run into a real pro who could show me the ropes."

I studied her curiously. "You're sure you want to get into this racket?"

She gave her head a vigorous nod. "I want nice clothes, and a big car, and all the other things money can buy. I'd learn fast. I promise."

I said, "Maybe we can help each other. As I told you, I've been looking for a girl like you. I need a partner for a pitch I'm working on."

"I'll be your partner," she said instantly.

I smiled at her. "Without even knowing what the dodge is?"

She looked a little embarrassed. "Do I sound too eager? I guess I am. But you don't know how scared I've been ever since I started this. What if I got caught, I kept wondering? I wished I had someone to work with, just for moral support. But all my friends are honest. They'd be horrified if they knew what I planned to do when I left for California. They all think I'm trying to get into the movies. I don't care what the job is. I'll do it."

14

"Not so fast," I said. "First I need answers to some questions."

"What questions?"

"To begin with, this *is* your first try, isn't it?"

She nodded.

"You have a record anywhere for anything else?"

She shook her head. "I've never tried anything else illegal."

"What made you decide to be a bunco artist?" I asked curiously.

She flushed again. In a low voice she said, "I got tired of working in a dime store. One night I saw this movie about an heiress running away from an arranged marriage. She met this fellow who was poor but honest. He didn't know she was an heiress. He helped her out because she was broke, and they fell in love. Then he discovered she was rich and it made him mad and he wouldn't have any more to do with her. He had principles, you see. But in the end he came around and decided he loved her in spite of her money, and her father came around too, and practically begged the hero to marry his daughter, and it all ended happily."

Fascinated, I said, "And that gave you the idea of becoming a con-woman?"

"Not right away. I daydreamed a little about being an heiress in disguise. Only I'd meet a rich man who was incognito too, and neither of us would discover the other was rich until after we were in love. Then I got to thinking, what if I went somewhere and just pretended to be an heiress? In the movie this poor boy spent half of the little he had to help the girl out. Why couldn't I find a rich man who would be willing to come to a runaway heiress's aid? I kept daydreaming about it

15

until finally the plan was all formed. So finally I decided to try it."

I grinned at her. "You should have written the plot down instead, and added a romantic ending. Maybe you could sell it to some women's magazine."

She said petulantly, "You're making fun of me again."

"Just trying to find out what makes you tick," I assured her. "Where are you from?"

She was from Chicago, she told me. She had a high-school education, plus a six-month business course. Her parents were dead. She had been working in the office of a dime store as a combination cashier, bookkeeper and file clerk. She had five hundred dollars in savings when she got her great idea. Transportation to California and some new clothing had made a considerable dent in this stake. When she checked into the Beverly-Wilshire that afternoon, she had a hundred and fifty left.

"At least one part of my act was real," she said. "I'm almost out of money."

Then she wanted to know about me. I told her I was thirty years old, had a year of college at Iowa State and was a Korean War vet. I said I was single and admitted I'd never held a job of any sort, except in the army, for more than three months. I told her I'd been a bunco artist ever since I got out of service, but discreetly didn't mention any of the jobs I'd pulled.

"Ever been caught?" she asked.

I shook my head. "I've had a few narrow squeaks. I'm not wanted anywhere."

"You think I'd make a good partner?"

I looked her up and down again. "I'm willing to try you out. With no future commitments. If this pitch works, we'll discuss the future later."

She accepted this gratefully. Her attitude was a little like that of a girl applying for a job and hoping she was making the right impression. She didn't even ask what her split would be.

She did finally get around to asking what the job was, though.

"The mark is an elderly widow named Mrs. Cora Hollingsworth," I told her. "She's staying here at the hotel. Her weakness is championing underdogs, and she's also an incurable romantic about young love. She's past the age where romance interests her personally. I've told her a sad story about a young stenographer who works in my office back in New York, and whose husband is one of the G.I. prisoners still interned by the Chinese Reds. Out of sympathy I've been pressuring the State Department to do something about getting him released. But all I get is excuses. Using my international business connections, I've learned that a little bribery among the officials of his prison camp could get him spirited into India. The Red officials want ten thousand dollars."

"Ten thousand!" Mavis said, starry-eyed. Then she looked puzzled. "You're supposed to be rich. Doesn't she wonder why you don't put up the money?"

"I'm a hard-headed businessman," I explained. "I'll exert what influence I can to help the girl get back her husband. But why should I donate ten thousand bucks to an employee I only know casually? I'm sympathetic, but not that generous. I haven't suggested that she pay the freight either, of course. I merely told her the story as a bit of human interest, and let it work on her sentiments."

"You think she'll come across?"

I shrugged. "She's outraged at the injustice of it

17

all. She wants the girl's address, so she can look her up the next time she gets to New York. She hasn't suggested handing *me* any money, but I think she'd give it to the girl if she listened to the story again from her. I've been stalling her with the story that I think the girl's vacation is coming up, and I remember her mentioning something about visiting an aunt out here. I'm supposed to have written my secretary to find out. Meantime I've been looking around for a woman to play the stenographer's role."

"I could do it," Mavis said eagerly. "I even know shorthand and typing."

"The first thing to do is get you out of the hotel," I told her. "Mrs. Hollingsworth flew to Las Vegas today, but she'll probably be back late tonight. And it wouldn't do for her to see you just yet. Suppose you go up and pack and check out. I'll meet you in the lobby in a half-hour. I'll drive you to another hotel, and after you're settled, we can discuss the rest of the plan."

Before driving Mavis to another hotel, I took her to a pawnshop in downtown Los Angeles and bought her a plain wedding band and an engagement ring set with a small chip diamond.

"This is all the jewelry I want you to wear," I told her. "Ditch that gawdy watch and fake emerald."

I registered her at the Sheraton. The rest of the afternoon and late into the evening we sat in her room while I drilled into her what she was to say and how she was to act when she met Mrs. Hollingsworth.

"Just be natural," I told her. "You're supposed to be a working girl. You *are* a working girl, or at least you were until recently, so the part doesn't call for any the-

18

atrical ability. For God's sake don't try to act. You haven't any talent."

"All right," she said in a wounded voice.

"Your name is Mary Applebee," I said. "Your husband's name is John Emery Applebee. He's twenty-six years old and, in civilian life, drives a bakery truck. You were married on April fourteenth, 1951, just before he left for Korea. He was a corporal in the 101st Infantry. The telegram informing you he was missing in action arrived on your first anniversary, April fourteenth, 1952. Later you got word that he was a POW. Got all that?"

"I think so," she said.

I made her repeat it over and over until it was memorized. I added further details of her background and her husband's and made her memorize them too. I covered every possible thing I thought Mrs. Hollingsworth might ask about.

"Don't volunteer any of this," I told her. "I don't want you reeling off data like a parrot. You're supposed to be shy. Just answer what she asks. If she throws a curve by coming up with something we haven't covered, can you ad lib?"

"Oh, yes," she assured me.

"Does your husband have any brothers or sisters?" I shot at her.

"An older brother named Walter," she said instantly. "He's in the Navy."

I nodded. "I guess you'll do. Now once more. Go over the whole thing."

She was letter perfect by the time I left. I told her to stick close to her room the next day, so that I could reach her by phone.

19

When I got back to the Beverly-Wilshire, I checked at the desk and learned that Mrs. Hollingsworth hadn't yet gotten back from Las Vegas. But apparently she got in late that night. At any rate she was in the coffee shop for breakfast at her usual time the next morning.

I paused at her table to ask, "Break the bank at Las Vegas?"

Looking up, she said, "Oh, good morning, Mr. Carter. No. I lost my usual fifty dollars and quit. I've never won yet. Will you join me?"

Cora Hollingsworth was a plump, good-natured woman in her late sixties with snow-white hair and a smooth, serene face. She had such regular habits, I knew exactly when to enter the coffee shop or dining room in order to "accidentally" meet her. We had become pretty friendly, but I had deliberately kept our relationship on a casual, tourist-acquaintance basis. I never attempted to see her except at mealtime, and even then I usually arranged to sit with her not more than one meal a day. The pitch I was working didn't require building a close association. I was banking on her sympathy for the young Applebees to put her in the mood for parting with ten thousand dollars. Beyond implanting in her mind that I was in a position to make proper arrangements for disbursing the ten thousand and getting young John Applebee freed, I made no attempt to impress her.

Pulling out a chair, I sat across from her and picked up a menu. Until I had ordered and my breakfast had been served, I listened to her account of her Las Vegas adventures.

When she finally ran out of stories, I said as though I had just thought of it, "By the way, I got a wire from my secretary last night. Mary Applebee is flying into

Los Angeles this evening. She's been instructed to phone me here."

"Oh?" Mrs. Hollingsworth said with immediate interest. "Can I meet her?"

"I suppose I can arrange it. I understand she plans to spend the night in L.A., then take a bus to her aunt's tomorrow. Her aunt lives somewhere in the San Fernando Valley." Then I said a little diffidently, "We've gotten to know each other pretty well, Mrs. Hollingsworth. May I speak frankly about something that's been on my mind?"

"Of course," she said.

"You've gotten yourself all worked up about this girl without even knowing her. It's an unfortunate situation, but it really isn't either your problem or mine. Don't go overboard."

"Why, what do you mean, Mr. Carter?"

"I suspect you're thinking of picking up the tab for these Commie blackmailers," I said bluntly. "It's a generous thought, but not a very wise one. Forget it."

I figured this was safe. Cora Hollingsworth was one of those people who tend to be ashamed of generous impulses, but whose resolve is only strengthened by common-sense advice against them. Her reaction convinced me it had been a shrewd move.

Coloring slightly, she protested, "Why the thought never entered my head, Mr. Carter. I'm just interested in meeting the girl."

CHAPTER III

MRS. HOLLINGSWORTH was so enthused about seeing
Mary Applebee that she insisted on meeting the plane.
This was a complication that wasn't very difficult to work
out. I phoned Mavis to get out to the International Air-
port in advance with her bags and post herself near
the proper gate. When she heard the announcement that
the plane she was supposed to be on had come in, she
could mingle with the passengers as they came out the
gate, so that it would appear that she had been on it.

"Be surprised to see me," I cautioned her. "You're
not supposed to know I'm meeting you."

Everything went smoothly. The plane came in on time
at 5:35 P.M. Mavis was properly surprised to see me.
Cora Hollingsworth was obviously charmed by her
fresh, innocent appearance.

Following the instructions I had given her over the
phone, Mavis said her plans were to stay overnight in
Los Angeles, as she couldn't get a bus out to her aunt's
until the next day. To avoid the possibility of Mrs.
Hollingsworth insisting she stay at the Beverly-Wilshire,
where the desk clerk knew Mavis by her real name, I
had told Mavis to say she had a reservation at a small,
moderately-priced hotel in downtown Los Angeles.

I took both women to the Statler, which is also in
downtown Los Angeles, for dinner.

Mavis put on a superb performance by simply being

herself. She seemed awed by the unexpected attention that she, a mere stenographer, was getting from one of the top executives of her company. She was equally awed by the Statler dining room, its headwaiter and by the prices on the menu. She respectfully addressed me as "sir." I was afraid she was going to overdo it by calling Mrs. Hollingsworth "ma'am," but she showed surprising discrimination now that she wasn't trying to be an heiress. Mrs. Hollingsworth was too maternal a type to awe anyone, and Mavis seemed to sense that with her it would be out of place not to be at ease. She struck exactly the right note by being respectful and just a little shy.

Her responses to Mrs. Hollingsworth's questions about her husband were flawless, too. She even amazed me by coming through when Mrs. Hollingsworth threw her a curve I hadn't anticipated.

It was as we were having coffee. Mrs. Hollingsworth had plied Mavis with sympathetic questions all during the meal. Now, all of a sudden, she asked, "Do you have a picture of your husband, Mary?"

My heart sank. It would be completely out of character for a woman as concerned over her imprisoned husband as Mary Applebee was supposed to be not to carry a picture of him. But I'd never thought of it. It was one of those vital minor details which can wreck the best-laid plans.

Mavis came through after only the barest hesitation. Opening her simulated alligator bag she drew out a wallet. From the wallet she produced a small portrait photograph of a good-looking young man about her own age.

"It's three years old," she said apologetically as she

23

handed it over. "It's been that long since we've seen each other."

Probably an ex-boyfriend, I thought with relief. It was fast thinking to remember it was in her wallet. I was proud of her.

"My, he's a nice-looking boy," Mrs. Hollingsworth said. "I don't blame you for wanting him back." She handed back the photograph. "Mr. Carter tells me a ten-thousand-dollar bribe would free him."

Mavis nodded and carefully tucked the photo away. "I save every cent I can. I wouldn't even have come down here if my aunt hadn't mailed me the ticket. But it will take years to save that much. About ten more, I figure." There was nothing forlorn in her voice. It contained a note of desperate determination.

Mrs. Hollingsworth stared at her thoughtfully. Then she glanced at me, cleared her throat and turned back to Mavis again. "I have a little money, dear. And I give heavily to charities all the time. There's no reason I couldn't do some personal charity work for a change."

Frowning at her, I gave my head a slight shake.

"You mind your business, Mr. Carter," she told me with spirit. "It's my money, and I'll do what I please with it." She returned to Mavis. "My dear, I'm going to put up the money to get your husband freed from that awful place."

Mavis's face turned radiant. "Honest? Oh, if you would, I'd thank you forever!"

I said reprovingly, "Mrs. Hollingsworth, I thought we agreed that this isn't your problem."

She gave me a haughty look. "It's certainly my money. Are you going to try to discourage me right in front of the child? She'll certainly think highly of you if you try to block the freeing of her husband."

"That's not fair," I protested. "Naturally I'd like to see Mary happy. I feel a certain responsibility here because I was the one who told you about her problem. I'm merely trying to protect your interests."

Deciding she had me on the defensive, Mrs. Hollingsworth followed up her advantage. "You should be protecting Mary's interests instead. She's an employee of yours, and I'm not. A thoughtful boss would put her welfare ahead of an outsider's. No wonder workers band into unions."

Mavis said eagerly, "It would only be a loan, Mr. Carter. John and I could pay it back, once he's home and both of us are working. Lots of couples owe more than that on a home. Oh, please, sir, let her."

"Let me, fiddlesticks," Mrs. Hollingsworth said. "I have sons older than your boss, child, and they don't tell me what to do. I don't need his permission. The matter's settled." She looked at me defiantly.

I gave a resigned shrug. "As you say, it's your money, Mrs. Hollingsworth."

"Hmph," she said. "Am I also going to have to go to China and make personal arrangements, or will you deign to use your connections to get the bribe placed in the proper hands there?"

Mavis looked at me appealingly. "You know what arrangements have to be made, sir. You'll take care of it, won't you?"

With a rueful smile I raised my hands in a gesture of defeat. "I won't argue any more. Mrs. Hollingsworth has placed me in the position of a villain trying to keep your husband imprisoned for some fiendish reason of my own. As long as she's determined to put up the money, I'll be glad to use my connections to have John freed. You understand, Mary, that I wasn't trying to discourage the loan because I'm unsympathetic. It's just—"

"It's just that Mr. Carter is a businessman," Mrs. Hollingsworth interrupted. "He doesn't understand that human values are more important than dollars and cents." She added for my benefit, in case I thought she was being too harsh with me, "Not that I don't like him. He's really quite charming, and probably a good boss in most ways. Don't think badly of him."

"Oh, I don't," Mavis said enthusiastically. "Tonight I think everybody is wonderful."

Again I was afraid she was going to overdo it, but she didn't. She didn't engulf Mrs. Hollingsworth with thanks. She acted as though she were too overwhelmed to express herself properly, which was a more effective thank-you than a lot of words would have been.

When we left the Statler, the elderly dowager said, "We'll drop you off at your hotel now, dear. You go on to your aunt's tomorrow and enjoy your vacation. I'll give Mr. Carter a check as soon as we get home, so he can start matters moving at once."

We dropped Mavis off in front of the small hotel she designated, and I drove back to the Beverly-Wilshire. Mrs. Hollingsworth asked me to stop by her room for a moment, wrote out a check for ten thousand dollars and handed it to me.

"Better phone your bank in the morning and tell them it's all right to cash this," I advised. "I'll want to exchange it for a cashier's check and get it off to New York at once."

She did phone the bank the next morning, and I had no trouble exchanging it for a cashier's check made out to myself.

Immediately afterward I checked out of the hotel, picked up Mavis and we headed for Las Vegas.

Mavis seemed strangely subdued. We were well on the way before I noticed it, though. When putting distance behind me after a job, I concentrate on the road ahead. We were fifty miles out of town before I grew conscious of her odd silence.

"What's the matter with you?" I inquired. "You ought to feel good. You did a beautiful job."

"I keep thinking about that old lady," she said. "She was such a nice person, Sam. I keep wondering what she'll think when she realizes we were crooks."

I frowned sidewise at her. "She won't miss the money. She's loaded. You know what the first major rule of this racket is?"

"What?"

"Never give a trimmed mark another thought. If you do, you won't sleep nights. If you're going to feel sorry for marks, you're in the wrong racket. Want to mail your share of the take back?"

"Oh, no," she said quickly. Her expression turned dreamy. "All that nice money. How many things it can buy! Don't worry about my conscience, Sam. As long as we can make money this easily, I'll subdue it."

"You sure you can?"

She gave a definite nod. "I promise I'll never think of the old lady again. Or any other mark, after a job."

"What makes you think there will be any more jobs?"

She gave me an anxious look. "Aren't you going to keep me with you? You said I did a beautiful job."

"You want to form a permanent partnership?" I asked.

"Oh, yes," she said eagerly. "I want to stick with you. Can I, Sam?"

"We'll see when we get where we're going," I said noncommittally.

We hit Las Vegas at two P.M. I converted the cashier's check into cash, and then sold my car to a used-car dealer on the off-chance that Mrs. Hollingsworth might remember the license number. Two hours after we arrived in Las Vegas, we were riding a plane toward Denver under assumed names.

We had dinner on the plane. When we landed, I had a taxi drive us directly to a small hotel on the outskirts of the city.

En route I glanced at Mavis's left hand, noted it was bare and asked, "What did you do with that wedding band and engagement ring?"

"They're in my bag," she said. "Why?"

"Put them on."

She gave me a puzzled look, but obeyed.

At the hotel I registered as Mr. and Mrs. Samuel Kinn of Houston, Texas. Mavis said nothing until the bellhop had deposited our bags in our room and departed. Then she thoughtfully regarded the double bed with which the room was furnished.

"Don't I even get asked?" she inquired.

I pulled a bottle of bourbon from one of my bags, set it on the dresser and phoned room service for soda and ice.

When I hung up, she said, "Don't I get answered either?"

"Sure," I said. "Didn't you say you wanted this to be a permanent partnership?"

"I was thinking of a business partnership."

"With me, it's all the way or not at all," I told her. "That's the way it is. You can still walk out."

Her lower lip stuck out petulantly. "You could be a little more romantic about it."

"I know how to be romantic," I assured her. "You'll be treated like a queen. I'm starting us off this way on purpose."

"Why?"

"Because I want you to have no doubt in your mind from the beginning about who's boss." I tapped my chest. "This guy is. In business, in bed, everywhere. I give the orders and you take them. You want to stay under my conditions, or take your cut and leave right now?"

She studied me for a moment more. "Do you have to make it an ultimatum?" she complained. "Couldn't you at least say you want me because I appeal to you as a woman?"

"If you didn't appeal to me as a woman, you'd be registered in another room." I crooked a finger at her. "Come here."

She hesitated, then warily moved toward me.

Pulling her against my chest, I wound my fingers in her black hair and jerked her head back. She put up a token struggle when I kissed her, but after a moment her arms slid about my neck. Her lips opened under mine and her body strained against me.

She whispered, "You can be boss, Sam. Everywhere."

Picking her up bodily, I tossed her on the bed. Her eyes grew wider and wider as I tossed my coat onto a chair, tossed my tie after it and began to strip off my shirt.

A knock came at the door. I had completely forgotten ordering ice and soda from room service.

CHAPTER IV

THE NEXT MORNING, I bought a nearly-new Mercury sedan, and we headed east. Two days later we hit St. Louis.

Our headlong flight halfway across the country was the unnecessary sort of blunder I never made in later years. Back then, the minute a deal was closed, I felt impelled to run. But there really had been no reason for haste in leaving Los Angeles. Mrs. Hollingsworth hadn't the slightest suspicion that she'd been taken. I could have stayed around for several more days, then announced that my vacation was over and I had to return to New York. Assuring the old woman that I'd keep her posted on developments probably would have postponed any suspicion on her part for weeks.

As it was, my sudden departure without even saying good-by must have aroused her suspicion at once. The wire service report of our bunco dodge reached St. Louis about the same time we did. It only got brief, inside-page coverage that far from Los Angeles, but it gave our descriptions and said we were wanted for fraud.

We were far enough away now to be reasonably safe, though. The police don't seem to hunt down bunco artists as relentlessly as they do more violent criminals, such as bank robbers. While it wouldn't be wise to return to California for some time, we didn't have to fear that every St. Louis policeman we saw would have our descriptions memorized and was on the lookout for us.

We checked into the Chase Hotel as Mr. and Mrs. Samuel Doud of Chicago and started to spend our money.

Mavis had the time of her life. It was the first time she had ever had all the shopping money she wanted. I turned her loose in the stores with instructions to outfit herself from head to toe.

The result was miraculous. Except for her liking for flashy jewelry, Mavis had excellent taste when she had the money to indulge it. In her new clothes she actually looked like an heiress.

I wouldn't let her buy any jewelry, not trusting her taste in that area. But I bought her some myself. I got her a plain, smart-looking wristwatch and a half-carat diamond ring to replace the chip she wore. I also got her a couple of expensive pins and a few sets of earrings. When I gave it all to her, she examined it dubiously.

"It's all very nice," she said. "But isn't it kind of plain?"

"That's the idea," I told her. "I want you to look like a lady, not a barroom pickup. From here on out you're never to wear any jewelry I don't personally select. Understand?"

"All right, Sam," she said reluctantly.

For a whole month we did nothing but play. Mavis made a delightful playmate. She was full of life, eager for new experiences, and as enthusiastic as a child at a circus whenever I took her anywhere. I took her to baseball games, fights, auto races, to Forest Park Highlands, and even to the zoo. We hit every show and every night club in town. We sampled every recreational facility St. Louis had to offer.

31

And we spent a lot of time simply making love. It was like being on a honeymoon.

Although I controlled the spending of money, had our local bank account in my name and wrote all checks, I took advantage of Mavis's bookkeeping experience by making her the family accountant. Near the end of June she balanced up my checkbook and announced, "You know we've gone through over five thousand dollars in only a month, Sam?"

"I'm not surprised," I said. "How do we stand?"

"About five thousand left. Didn't you have anything when we met?"

"About what you did," I said. "Under two hundred. I hadn't made a score for some time."

Actually Cora Hollingsworth was the first *big* score I'd ever managed to pull off. My stake before meeting Mavis had never climbed over a couple of thousand. But I didn't tell her that.

Mavis was frowning down at the paper containing her computations. "At this rate we'll be broke in another month, Sam. Shouldn't we start economizing?"

"I like to live high," I told her. "It's time to go back to work."

We started that same evening. I brought out my potential sucker list and went over it.

My sucker list had been compiled over a number of years from numerous sources. From newspaper reports of top income-tax payers, from inheritance reports, from *Who's Who,* from magazine articles on prominent people, from the society pages of major city newspapers and from the bunco-game grapevine, which stretches from coast-to-coast and keeps members of the fraternity informed as to what marks have recently been taken, and how, and constantly adds new prospects to the **list.** For every large city in the country I had a list of **at** least a dozen possibles.

From my St. Louis list I picked a couple of rich widows, a widower and a prominent society matron who was noted as a patroness of struggling young artists.

"Four possibles," I said. "We'll start weeding them out tomorrow."

"How?" Mavis asked.

"The newspaper morgues. We compile all the background material we can on all four. Then pick the one we figure has the kindest heart."

"Are we going to try the same stunt we pulled in Los Angeles?"

"If any of the possibles have a weakness for sad stories. If not, we'll dream up some angle to take advantage of whatever weaknesses they have. If none have any that seem promising, we'll move on to some other city."

The next morning I visited the *Post Dispatch* and Mavis went to the *Globe Democrat*. The story that we were magazine writers doing research for some personality pieces got us into both morgues without difficulty. At noon we met to compare notes.

We settled on one of the widows, a Mrs. Sarah Brewster. She gave heavily to charity and did a lot of personal welfare work, such as delivering baskets to the poor at Christmastime. She sounded like a carbon copy of Mrs. Cora Hollingsworth.

Mrs. Brewster was a permanent resident at the Jefferson Hotel. I moved in there, leaving Mavis at the Chase, and within a week had her lined up for the kill with the same dodge we had used in California. Three days later we blew town with eight thousand dollars of Mrs. Brewster's money.

Mrs. Brewster had been just as nice an old lady as Cora Hollingsworth. But if Mavis suffered any conscience pangs this time, she managed to suppress them. The only emotion she exhibited was glee at the ease with which we had extracted the money.

During the next six months we pulled the same pitch twice again, once in Pittsburgh and once in Seattle. We had a close call in Seattle. As I came out of the bank after cashing the mark's check, I bought a morning paper. On its front page was a warning against the racket we had just pulled, along with a resume of our scores in Beverly Hills, St. Louis and Pittsburgh.

I didn't wait to get out of town before converting the cashier's check into cash. I cashed it at a bank three blocks from the first, picked up Mavis and we took off fast. Apparently our mark didn't read the morning paper, for we squeaked through without running into any road blocks.

We stopped in Salt Lake City long enough to sell the car, and flew from there to Houston, Texas.

We decided to lay low in Houston for a while. We now had a fifteen-thousand-dollar stake and, even with our taste for high living, could afford a lengthy vacation.

We spent Christmas at the Shamrock Hotel. Christmas Eve, possibly under the influence of the season, I asked Mavis to marry me.

We were in the Shamrock's cocktail lounge having an after-dinner drink when I asked her. She paused with her drink half raised and slowly set it down again. Her green eyes were bright when she looked at me, but there was an odd, waiting expression on her face. She didn't make any answer. She just continued to stare at me.

"Didn't you hear me?" I said. "I asked how you'd like to get married."

"I heard you," she said. "I was just wondering why."

"Why I asked you?"

"Why you want to marry me."

I frowned at her. "We're living as man and wife anyway. We make a perfect business team. As far as I'm concerned, it's a permanent relationship. Why not make it legal?"

She smiled a little ruefully. "All perfectly logical reasons."

"What's the matter with you?" I inquired. "Don't you want to get married?"

"There isn't anything I'd like more," she assured me. "I happen to be in love with you."

"Then why all the shilly-shallying?"

She lifted her shoulders in a resigned shrug. "You reeled off three sensible reasons for wanting to marry me. None of them the one reason every woman wants to hear."

I examined her dubiously. Women are such incurable romantics. "You mean I haven't said I love you?"

"Not ever," she informed me. "Not since the day we met. You treat me like you love me, most of the time. You act proud of me in public. You hardly ever fail to tell me how nice I look when we start out. And in bed— well, you don't act as though I repel you. But not once, ever, have you said those corny little words: I love you."

"I'm just not demonstrative," I said. "Of course I love you. Satisfied?"

She gave me a wry smile. "What woman wouldn't be after such a passionate avowal?"

"Don't be sarcastic," I said impatiently. "You want to get married or not?"

"You're the boss in this family," she said. "We do whatever you want to do."

We were married on New Year's Day. We took a six-week honeymoon cruise to South America, then returned to Houston and stretched our honeymoon to another six weeks at the Shamrock.

Toward the end of March, Mavis announced that we had a little over four thousand dollars left in the bank. It was time to go back to work.

"We have to dream up a new racket," I told Mavis. "The POW gimmick has about worn itself out. Let's see what the Houston sucker list has to offer."

The Houston list turned up two old ladies who would have been perfect marks for the prisoner-of-war dodge. But I was afraid of it. Our previous scores had been too well publicized.

"I don't see a single weakness we might capitalize on among these other people," I told Mavis. "There's a guy who collects stamps, another who's a nut on sailboating. There's a couple of women who spend all their time at club meetings. Period. Give me a couple of days to think."

It was Mavis who finally produced an idea, though I was the one to recognize it as a possibility. She was reading the paper in bed one morning while I shaved, when she suddenly emitted a little laugh.

"Listen to this, honey," she called through the open bathroom door. "People put some of the funniest things in personal ads."

"Yeah?" I inquired.

"Comely widow, age 35, desires correspondence with single or widowed gentleman of same age. Must be strong, healthy, willing to work, able to manage fight gym left by deceased husband. Object: matrimony."

I grinned into the mirror and went on shaving. "The world is full of screwballs," I said. "How about phoning room service for breakfast?"

For some reason the item stuck in my mind. As we lingered over our breakfast coffee, I said, "Wonder if that widow has any money in addition to the gym."

"The one in the ad?" Mavis inquired.

"Yeah," I said. "See if you can find that item again."

Mavis rose to get the paper and began to turn pages. "Here it is," she said finally, handing me the folded paper and pointing out the item.

I read it over, noting that a box number was given for replies.

"It says she's a *comely* widow," I commented. "According to Webster, that means agreeable to the sight."

"That's her own description," Mavis said. "She's probably a living horror. If she wasn't, she wouldn't have to advertise for a husband."

"There's one way to find out."

Mavis raised her eyebrows inquiringly.

"I'm going to answer the ad," I told her. "Maybe she has some money we can shake loose."

I didn't know it at the time, but my decision was the turning point of our lives. It was to start us in a new and permanent career.

It was our entry into the big time.

CHAPTER V

Mavis pointed out that the ad asked for a man of thirty-five, and I had just passed my thirty-first birthday in February.

"Of course, some men don't change much between thirty and forty," she said. "Maybe you could pass for a young-looking thirty-five."

I went to look in a mirror, and decided I could.

Mavis and I spent a lot of time drafting a letter. We were pretty proud of the finished product. It went:

Dear Madam:

This is in answer to your personal ad in this morning's paper. I am a single man of thirty-five with no relatives except a younger sister. I believe I have all the qualifications to manage a fight gymnasium.

I had two years of college at the State University of Iowa, majoring in physical education. I was on the university boxing team both years. Later, for seven years, I was an athletic trainer and faculty manager of the boxing team. For the past three years I have been a fight trainer in New York State. Recently the owner and manager of the training camp where I worked died, and the camp was sold to a man who converted it into a vacation resort. I am therefore free of any commitments at the moment.

I am six feet three, weigh 210 and have a fairly presentable appearance.

Any matrimonial discussion would have to await our meeting and getting to know each other, of course. But even if this didn't work out, perhaps we could come to a business agreement about managing your gymnasium.

> Very truly yours,
> Samuel Plainfield.

I thought that the Shamrock would be an unlikely address for a man answering a matrimonial ad. I rented a post office box and gave its number as my return address.

Two days later I got an answer. It read:

Dear Mr. Plainfield:

I got your letter. You sound like a good prospect. Now let me tell you about me.

My husband has been dead six months, and the guys running the gym he left me are robbing me blind. I could sell it, but it brings a pretty good income when it's run right, and I'd have to take a gypping if I let it go right now when its income is down. Not that I really need its income, because my husband left me pretty well fixed besides the gym. But I'm tired of being robbed. I'm also tired of sleeping alone, if you get what I mean. I'm the kind of woman who needs a man around.

Like I said in the ad, I'm thirty-five, too. And not a bad looker, if you like them a little on the plump side. I'm five feet four and weigh 142 pounds. I can knock off twenty pounds with hardly no effort at all with a diet I got, though, if you like them slimmer.

Like you, I don't want to buy no pig in a poke, so I'm not promising anything until we meet. But if you'd like to talk it over, come out to the house any evening after seven P.M.

Yours truly,
Mrs. Hannah Stokes.

The return address was in the thirty-nine hundred block of Case, which is a solid, upper-middle-class residential section.

Mavis said, "She sounds like a dream. I think I'm jealous."

"You should be," I said dryly. "She has so much more than you do."

"Probably all in the wrong places," Mavis murmured. "I hope."

I had some preparations to make before I called on Mrs. Hannah Stokes. All of the clothes I owned would have been as out of character as my Shamrock address. I went down to a department store and bought a cheap ready-made suit, a pair of cheap shoes and a dollar necktie.

When I called on the widow that evening, I looked like what I was supposed to be: a man of moderate income all dressed up for a blind date. I arrived at five minutes after seven.

Hannah Stokes lived in a two-story frame home with a broad lawn edged by a low fence. The door opened instantly when I rang.

The woman had lied a little about her age. She looked close to forty. She was a stocky, freckle-faced woman with wide hips and a massive bust. In a coarse sort of way she wasn't bad-looking. She had strawberry-blonde hair that fell to her shoulders in waves, a wide, humorous mouth and twinkling brown eyes in a plain, but not unattractive, face, and strong white teeth. She was solid rather than fat, having a moderate waistline and well-rounded, though somewhat thick, arms and legs.

Apparently she had prepared for company in case it came. She wore a loud print dress, a rhinestone bracelet with matching earrings, bright lipstick and mascara.

"Mrs. Stokes?" I asked.

"Yeah," she said, examining me with a mixture of approval and hope.

"I'm Sam Plainfield."

"Well," she said enthusiastically. "You're better looking than I ever hoped. Come on in."

She led me into a garishly-furnished front room, took my hat and coat and invited me to sit down. I chose an easy chair. She draped my wraps over another chair and plumped herself onto the sofa. She looked at me expectantly.

"You have a nice home," I commented. "You live here all alone?"

She nodded. "Gaylord and me never had no children. That was my husband, Gaylord. He wanted some, but nothing ever happened. It wasn't me, because I went to a doctor and found out I was okay. Gaylord wouldn't go for a check. I think he was afraid he'd find out he shot blanks."

She was refreshingly frank, I thought. I said, isn't it rather expensive to keep up this big a place just for yourself?"

"I figure on having a husband sharing it before long," she said. "Anyhow, it's all clear. Gaylord left me pretty well-fixed. He dropped dead of a heart attack just six months ago last Friday."

I gave a sympathetic murmur.

"Oh, don't feel sorry about it," she said. "If he hadn't, I wouldn't be nearly so well-fixed. It was mostly insurance money. The gym was clear and this house was clear, but we didn't have a dime in the bank."

"He was heavily insured, eh?"

"We both was. Gaylord believed in insurance. There's twenty thousand on me, too. Paid up life. He took it out when he was first married twent—fifteen years ago." She caught herself just in time. She had almost given away her true age.

I said, "I didn't realize you were so well-off. I'm afraid I haven't that much to offer. I have a little in savings, but I'm not a rich man."

"I got enough for both of us," she said with a grin. "In case we get together. How come you're still single at thirty-five, Sam?"

Apparently we were going to be on a first-name basis from the start. I said, "I guess I just never met the right girl, Hannah."

She gave me an arch look. "Think maybe you finally have? Or am I going too fast for you? I'm a great one for snap judgements."

"Oh?"

"Minute I opened the door and saw you, I flipped. If I'm going too fast, you'll just have to get used to me, because that's the way I am. I'll tell you right out, you're what I've been looking for. I'm willing to head for a J.P. right now."

I grinned at her. "Without knowing a thing about me?

42

There's an old axiom that goes, 'Marry in haste, repent at leisure.' "

"What more do I have to know?" she inquired. "You're a college man. I never in the world expected to hear from no college man. You must be steady or you wouldn't have that Iowa job for seven years. Losing the one up in New York wasn't your fault if the place went out of business. And you're a living doll. I'm all set." Then she looked concerned. "Or don't you like me?"

"I think you're wonderful," I said sincerely. "But you kind of sweep me off my feet. Let's get a little better acquainted before we make any final decisions."

"I knew I was going too fast," she said agreeably. "I'm like that. Whatever you say. How shall we start getting acquainted?"

"Well, first, if you expect me to manage your gym, why don't you tell me about it?"

She told me about it in detail. It was in downtown Houston and was used mainly by professional fighters in training. While her husband was alive, the income from it had supported them, paid for their home and paid the premiums on the heavy insurance they both carried. Since his death, two of the employees were jointly managing it, and the income had fallen off to half. She was convinced they were robbing her.

"I figure with a husband to manage it again, income will jump right back to where it was," she said. "So, really, he'll be paying his way. We could live on the gym and not even have to touch the insurance money except for something special, like maybe a honeymoon. You want to take a look at the gym tonight? There won't be nobody there at this time, but I got keys."

I wasn't anxious to be seen by any more people who

knew her than necessary. A visit to the place tonight would give me an excuse for postponing future visits when it was open. I agreed that it would be a good idea.

I had bought another car when we first arrived in Houston, this time a year-old Plymouth. We drove down to the gymnasium in it.

It was a typical fighter's gym, a big, barnlike structure whose main room contained a ring plus all the training paraphernalia fighters use. In addition, there was a locker room with showers, a rubdown room and an office. I looked it over with a show of interest I didn't feel, as I had no intention of ever managing it.

"Pretty fair equipment," I told her in a professional tone. "You need a new heavy bag and a couple more punching bags, though."

"Well, that'd be your problem if we get together," Hannah said. "I don't know beans about the business. You'd be in full charge."

When we got back to the house, she invited me in again. As before, we sat in the front room.

"Anything else you want to know?" she asked.

I asked her a few more questions about herself, and she answered them in detail. She had no relatives closer than uncles, aunts and cousins, I learned, and none of them lived in Texas. She had only a grade-school education, but assured me she read all the time. Her favorite magazine was *True Story*.

She didn't ask me a single thing, even how I happened to be in Texas when my last job was in New York State. As long as she was willing to take me at face value, I didn't offer any information.

At eleven I rose to leave.

"Do you have to take off so early?" she asked wistfully.

"It'll be midnight when I get back to the motel," I said. "We can get together again tomorrow."

Rising from the sofa, she watched disconsolately as I pulled on my coat. "I got lots of room here," she said. "There's three bedrooms upstairs. You could save all that drive home and back again tomorrow."

I cocked an eyebrow at her. "Wouldn't the neighbors talk?"

"Aw, who cares about the neighbors? They hardly speak to me anyhow. They're all uppity around here. Anyhow, if we're going to be married, what difference would a few days or weeks make?"

I couldn't keep an amused expression from forming on my face. Hannah had the grace to blush.

"There I go again," she said. "Always going too fast. But you said we ought to get acquainted. I don't know a better way for a man and woman to get acquainted in a hurry."

I considered the invitation. There wasn't much doubt in my mind that if I took it, I could have her eating out of my hand by morning. There also wasn't much doubt in my mind that I was going to have to climb into bed with her eventually, if I expected to get hold of any of her money. She wasn't the type of woman who would turn her life savings over to a lover who merely whispered sweet nothings in her ear.

She wasn't what I would have picked as a bed partner for pure enjoyment, but she wasn't repulsive either. There was a robust sexuality about her that was kind of appealing. And at least she was clean. She had the freshly-scrubbed appearance of a woman who used lots of soap regularly.

I said, "The sister I mentioned in my letter is down

45

here with me. She might worry if I stayed out all night."

"Call her up," Hannah urged. "Give her some story."

I pretended to muse. I had mentioned the sister only as an excuse not to spend the entire night.

"She's in a separate cabin at the motel," I said. "She wouldn't know I wasn't in until morning. Suppose I just stay for a couple of hours, and then go home?"

Hannah looked pleased at this concession. "All right," she agreed. "We can do a lot of getting acquainted in a couple of hours. Give me your coat again."

She wasn't bad. What she lacked in finesse, she more than made up for in enthusiasm.

I got back to the Shamrock at 4:00 A.M.

CHAPTER VI

Mavis was asleep when I got in, but my switching on the light awakened her. Sitting up, she glanced at her watch and gave me an inquiring look.

"It looks good," I said. "She's around forty and wants a man so bad, she's ready to do anything to get one. She decided she wanted to marry me two minutes after we met."

I started to undress.

"Does she have any money?" Mavis asked.

"Her husband left some insurance. I didn't ask how much, but she implied it was twenty thousand at least."

Mavis's eyes lit up. "Have you worked out a plan yet?"

"Not yet," I said. "But she's overboard enough to rise to almost anything. I'll dream up some kind of an investment for her."

Mavis watched as I hung my suit up. "Is she pretty?" she asked finally.

"She's forty, or close to it, and weighs a hundred forty-two pounds."

"She could still be pretty," Mavis said. "They say Venus di Milo weighed a hundred and forty."

"Standards of beauty have changed since then," I told her. "You can see for yourself tomorrow. You're going to meet her. I told her my sister was with me. Incidentally, she thinks we're staying in a motor court. We'll have to move to one tomorrow. Do you still have the outfit you wore when we met?"

"Of course. I've worn it every time I played Mary Applebee."

"Wear it again tomorrow," I said. "We're supposed to be in the middle-income class."

I switched out the light and climbed into bed. Mavis moved to snuggle in my arms. "Love me?" she asked.

"Uh-huh."

Her arms went about my neck and she pressed her body against mine.

"Not tonight," I said. "I'm worn to a frazzle."

The next morning we checked out of the Shamrock and moved to a motel. I had Mavis remove her wedding band and engagement ring. We registered in separate cabins as Samuel Plainfield and Miss Mavis Plainfield.

I had arranged to take Hannah to lunch and introduce her to my "sister." We arrived at the house at noon, and I took Mavis inside with me. Mavis looked relieved when she saw the woman, deciding she wasn't even in the running as competition. Why she had been worried in the first place, I don't know, because even before she met Hannah, she knew she had a fifteen-year youth advantage.

Hannah greeted her politely, asked how she liked Houston, then inquired what had brought Mavis down there. This surprised me a little, as she hadn't even asked me that. She hadn't asked me anything at all, as a matter of fact, apparently being so overwhelmed by my appearance in her life that she was afraid questioning her good luck might awaken her from her dream and cause me to disappear.

Mavis said, "When Sam came down here, I just decided

to come along. So I quit my job. I figured I wouldn't have any trouble getting another one here. I'm a trained stenographer."

I took both women to a moderately-priced restaurant downtown for lunch.

In Mavis's presence Hannah was a little more subdued than she'd been the previous night. She didn't even mention marriage. But she kept her bright eyes on me constantly, and there was a proprietory air about her that I could tell rankled Mavis a little.

Mavis didn't show it, however. On the surface she was politely friendly to the woman. Hannah failed to detect the slight edginess beneath the surface politeness. As a matter of fact, she paid little attention to Mavis after their brief conversation at the house. She was too wrapped up in me.

After lunch we dropped Mavis off to do some shopping, and Hannah and I went back to her house for further discussion. The minute the door closed behind us, the woman flew into my arms. It was apparent we weren't going to get any discussing done in the front room. I gave in gracefully and took her upstairs.

Later, lying side-by-side in bed, we finally got around to future plans. Hannah was all set to apply for a marriage license the moment I said the word.

"I think you're the woman I've been looking for, Hannah," I told her. "But I still think we ought to wait a short time until we're both sure."

"I'm sure," she said, leaning over to give me a resounding smack on the cheek. "But you take all the time you want, honey."

I said, "The only thing that bothers me is I don't like

the idea of living on a woman. I've only got a couple of thousand bucks. And you've got so much more."

Her huge bosom pushed against my chest as she snuggled up against me. "You'll pay your way by running the gym, Sam. Don't worry about it."

"You'll still have all the money," I said. "You own the house, the business, and you have the bank account."

"I won't after we're married, honey. With me marriage is fifty-fifty. Gaylord and I always had everything in both our names. With you and me it's gonna be the same. We split right down the middle. I'll have a lawyer put half the business and half the house in your name. And change the rest that Gaylord left me over the same way."

I said, "That insurance money ought to be invested instead of just lying idle in a bank."

"It's drawing good interest, honey."

"Not what solid, gilt-edged securities would draw. I have a broker friend in New York who knows the market inside out. With ten or twenty thousand capital, I could build a fortune in a year."

"Gaylord always said to stay clear of the stock market," she said disapprovingly. "Neither one of us went for gambling."

"There's a difference between investment and gambling, Hannah."

"Well, we'll talk about that after we're married," she said. "No point even discussing it till then."

I spent the rest of the day and that evening with Hannah. We dined at the house, as she said she wanted to demonstrate how well she could cook. She could, too. She served a delicious meal.

Several times I swung the conversation back to the subject of investments, but each time got the same firm answer. Despite her eagerness to get married, there was a grain of hard common sense in her. I'd been over-optimistic in thinking that merely taking her to bed would make her putty in my hands. Obviously she had no intention of loosening up with a single nickel until she had me safely married.

I got back to the motel about midnight to find Mavis waiting in my cabin. A freshly-opened bottle of whisky with about two ounces gone stood on the dresser next to a bowl of melting ice. Mavis was nursing the dregs of a highball. The ashtray next to her contained a half-dozen lipstick-stained butts. She had been waiting for some time.

She watched silently as I mixed myself a drink, then drained the last sip from her glass and held it out. I made her one too.

She sampled it before asking, "Any progress?"

I said, "It's going to be tougher than I expected. It looks as though she has no intention of loosening up until after we're married."

Mavis frowned. "What are you going to do?"

I took a large swallow of my drink. "I thought that over on the way home. There's only one thing to do."

"What?"

"Marry her," I said.

Mavis's eyes grew wide. "Bigamy?"

"Why not? It'd be under a fake name. It wouldn't affect the legality of our marriage even if I used my own name."

"But you'd have to *sleep* with her," Mavis protested.

I frowned at her. "This is business, Mavis. Don't go sentimental on me."

"Would you let me sleep with another man to work a dodge?" she demanded.

"I'd knock your head off if you suggested it," I growled at her. "It's not the same thing. And besides, you think I look forward to sleeping with the woman? You've seen what she's like. It's just business."

"Monkey business," she said hotly. "I won't have it."

I took a sip of my drink, eyeing her coldly over the edge of my glass. When I lowered it again, I asked ominously, "You're giving me orders?"

She flushed. "I mean, I don't want it. I'm asking you, Sam."

I said bluntly, "You're a little late. We've already been in bed together. In fact we haven't been much of anywhere else except to the gym last night and to lunch today. When Hannah said in her letter that she was tired of sleeping alone, it was an understatement. She seems determined to make up for each month of widowhood in a day."

Mavis's face turned white. She said nothing.

"I had to," I said roughly. "There was no other way to loosen her up. I'm not going to pass up twenty grand just because you're jealous. You think I like making love to a fat, middle-aged slob?"

She still said nothing.

"Keep in mind who's the boss in this family," I advised her. "I give the orders and you take them. We'll play this my way, and you'll like it."

Mavis gave her head a slow shake. Her face was still dead white. "We'll play it your way, if you insist, Sam. You're the boss. But you could beat me till I bled and I wouldn't like it."

"When did I ever beat you?" I asked ironically.

"Never physically," she said in a low voice.

The next day I told Hannah I had decided I wanted

to get married. We had our blood tests that same afternoon. This was a Friday, and we set the date for the following Wednesday. Hannah made no objecton when I insisted on a quiet ceremony before a J.P. with Mavis as the only witness.

She also made no objection when I suggested Mavis live with us for a short time until she could find work and was able to afford her own apartment.

"It will be nice to have someone look after the house while we're on a honeymoon, anyway," Hannah said. "We're going to take one, aren't we?"

I told her we would if she liked. Hannah decided she would like a two-week trip to New Orleans.

Once during the few days before the wedding, Hannah inquired if I would like to make a daytime visit to the gymnasium and meet the personnel who would be my employees when I took over its management. I told her there would be plenty of time for that after we returned from the honeymoon, and she didn't press the matter.

We were married as scheduled, Mavis standing up with us as the witness. As a wedding present I gave Hannah a twenty-five-dollar gold-filled bracelet and earring set. She waited to give me my wedding present until after we had returned to the house. Mavis didn't see it, as she went directly to her room and left us alone the moment we walked in the house.

Hannah opened the drawer of a writing table in the front room and produced three documents. She handed them to me with a smile.

One was a deed to the house made out jointly to Samuel Plainfield and Mrs. Hannah Plainfield. The second was a deed to the gymnasium made out the same way.

The third was a twenty-thousand-dollar paid-up life insurance policy on Hannah with a rider attached to it naming the insured's husband, Samuel Plainfield, as the beneficiary.

"That was still made out to Gaylord before I had it changed," she said. "If I'd dropped dead, I guess it would've just gone into the estate."

I gave her a thank-you kiss.

"There's more," she said. "I told you everything would be fifty-fifty. Let's go down to the bank."

I drove her downtown to her bank. Inside, she led me to the safety-vault room, signed in and we were admitted through the gate to the vault. Checking the card Hannah had signed, the attendant located the proper box and inserted the master key. After inserting her key also, Hannah drew out a long, narrow, lidded box.

I followed as she carried the box to one of the curtained cubbyholes provided for renters of safety-deposit boxes.

Opening the lid, she drew out a stack of government bonds and proudly handed them to me. There were twenty-four of them, each with a maturity value of a thousand dollars. I did some fast mental arithmetic and figured out that their purchase price would have been eighteen thousand. As they were dated only six months previously, their present value wasn't much more, and they wouldn't mature for nine and a half more years.

The bulk of the insurance money, I thought, and wondered what she had done with the other two thousand.

She answered the mental question without my having to ask it aloud. "I've got two thousand in a checking account too," she said. "You told me you had a couple of thousand, so you keep that in a checking account under your own name, and we'll be exactly even. Did you see how the bonds are made out?"

I looked at them again. They were co-owner bonds, made out to Hannah and Samuel Plainfield. Not to Hannah and/or Samuel Plainfield. She had arranged things so that it would take both our signatures to cash them.

I said, "Shouldn't I have a key to the box?"

"What for?" she asked. "There's nothing in it but the bonds. And it takes both of us to cash them. We'll have to be together to cash them when they mature anyway. One key's enough."

I said a little faintly, "When they mature? I thought we were going to discuss investing the insurance money in some stocks."

"Stocks, hell!" she said earthily. "Government bonds are safe. They're staying right where they are for another nine and a half years."

She meant it, I realized. She wasn't nearly the sucker I had imagined. I don't think she had the slightest suspicion that I was trying to take her. It was just innate good business sense that had caused her to arrange things to make it impossible. Everything was half in my name, but it would take her signature as well as mine to convert any of it into cash. And it was pretty obvious that even my most persuasive talking was never going to get her signature in agreement to sell anything.

It developed that she had made one more legal arrangement to tie everything up nicely. When we got back to the car, she asked me to drive her to her lawyer's office.

"What for?" I asked.

"I had him draw up a couple of wills, honey. Mine

55

leaves everything to you, yours leaves everything to me."

"That was generous of you," I said dubiously.

"Just good business," she said. "What if you dropped dead tomorrow? Your sister might inherit everything I just signed over to you. That wouldn't be fair."

I agreed that it wouldn't. There wasn't any logical reason I could give for refusing to sign a will, so I drove to her lawyer's.

He was a relatively young man, and apparently Hannah had told him all about me, because he seemed to know about the plan for me to run the gym. He warmly congratulated me on our marriage and wished Hannah happiness. If he suspected from our difference in ages that I had married her for her money, there was no indication of it in his manner.

He had both wills already drawn up. We each signed, and his office girl signed as a witness.

In bed that night, lying next to the snoring Hannah and thinking of Mavis lying alone, and probably sleepless, just down the hall, I ruefully considered the predicament I had worked myself into. All that tantalizing wealth half in my name, and I couldn't touch a cent of it.

There was one thing all in my name, though. The insurance policy.

I went to sleep on that thought.

CHAPTER VII

WE WERE SCHEDULED to leave on our honeymoon at noon the next day. I rose first and was showered, shaved and dressed before Hannah got up. Mavis was up too, and already downstairs. I had a chance to talk to her while Hannah was showering and dressing.

Mavis was seated in the kitchen over a cup of coffee and a cigarette when I came in. Dark circles under her eyes suggested she hadn't slept well, and she looked cool and remote. Silently she poured me a cup of coffee and pushed sugar and cream toward me.

I said, "You look as though you were awake all night."

"I kept listening for the creak of bedsprings from your room," she said sardonically. "Enjoy your wedding night?"

"Let's not squabble," I told her. "We haven't much time to talk before Hannah gets down."

"What's there to talk about?" she said listlessly.

"I've got a plan. It's pretty risky. Riskier than anything we've done yet. But it's the only way I can see to salvage anything from this mess."

"Oh, you agree it's a mess, do you?" Mavis said.

"Stop heckling and listen," I said impatiently. I told her how Hannah had tied everything up so I couldn't touch it without her signature.

Mavis thought for a moment when I finished. "Couldn't

you steal her safe-deposit box key?" she asked. "Get the bonds and forge her signature to them?"

I gave her a disgusted look. "Your signature card has to be on file before you can get through the vault gate. If I left planning to you, we'd have been bankrupt or in jail long ago. I'm not asking you for advice. I just want you to listen."

Mavis looked wounded. "All right. Go ahead."

I said, "If Hannah dies, I inherit everything. We'd not only get the insurance money and the bonds, we could sell the house and gym. Even a quick sale ought to bring fifteen thousand apiece from them."

Mavis's eyes started to widen, and grew wider and wider.

"Figure it up," I said. "Twenty thousand in insurance, eighteen thousand in bonds, two thousand in her checking account. If we got fifteen apiece for the house and gym, the total comes to seventy grand."

"But murder!" Mavis whispered.

"Yeah," I said. "Is it worth the risk? It's seventy grand or nothing. If you don't want to go along, we may as well take off right now. There's no point in wasting my time going on a honeymoon."

Mavis licked her lips. "Seventy thousand," she said in an unsteady voice.

"Or nothing. Make up your mind fast. Hannah will be down in a minute."

"How would we do it?" she asked.

"I haven't tried to work out any details yet. That's not important at this point, and anyway, we haven't time to discuss it now. What's important is will you go along?"

"You've never asked me if I'd do anything before," Mavis said. "You just told me."

"This is different," I said. "This is the big step. Maybe I haven't the guts to take it on my own. Maybe I need your moral support. I don't know. But I do know that if you don't want to go along, we're kicking the whole deal right now. We'll go up and pack, tell Hannah it's all off and leave."

Mavis looked at me from wide, frightened eyes. "I'd rather have you just tell me, Sam. I'm not used to making even little decisions. Don't throw one like this at me. I'll do what you say."

The bathroom door slammed upstairs.

"I'm not going to order you," I said urgently. "You're going to have to say one way or the other. I want this to be equal responsibility."

"How do you feel?" she asked.

"If I wasn't willing to go through with it, I wouldn't have brought the matter up," I said impatiently. "Make up your mind."

Mavis took a deep breath and let it out slowly. "If it was just murder for money, I don't think I could. If it was somebody like Mrs. Hollingsworth or Mrs. Brewster, for instance. Even for that much money."

When she paused, I growled, "Well?"

Her nostrils flared and she said in a suddenly vicious voice, "I hate her. I've been wishing she was dead since the moment you told me you'd made love to her. I'll go along, Sam."

Hannah's footsteps sounded on the stairs.

"We'll have to get together to plan it out," I said hurriedly. "Here's what we'll do. I'll arrange to have some car trouble when we hit Beaumont, so we'll have to spend the night there. As soon as Hannah and I leave, you run downtown and rent a car. Drive to Beaumont and register at the Hotel Beaumont under the name of Arlene Drake. I'll meet you there as soon as I can. Got it?"

Mavis nodded.

A moment later, when Hannah entered the kitchen with a cheery hello, we both had coffee cups raised to our lips.

Hannah and I got started at noon, as scheduled. Fifty miles out of town I stopped for gasoline and, as I expected, Hannah took advantage of the stop to visit the gas-station rest room. When she was gone, and while the attendant was at the back of the car filling the tank, I opened the hood, ostensibly to check the oil, and loosened a spark plug wire.

The car started to miss as soon as we pulled away from the gas station. Hannah looked at me inquiringly.

"Sounds like the fuel pump is going out," I said with a frown. "I should have had a checkup before we left."

By the time we reached the outskirts of Beaumont, the engine was missing badly.

I said, "Afraid we're going to have to stop for a new fuel pump. It'll probably take awhile to install. We may as well spend the night in Beaumont. We aren't in any hurry, are we?"

"Not me," Hannah said cheerfully. "I don't care where I am, so long as I'm with you."

I told her there was no point in her coming along and having to stand around in a repair garage while the car was being fixed. I suggested we find a motel, check in, and she could wait there in comfort while I saw to the car.

"All right," she said agreeably. "I brought along a couple of *True Stories* I can read."

We registered at a motel just inside of town. I left Hannah there and drove on into town, ostensibly in search of a repair garage.

As soon as I was out of sight of the motel, I pulled over to the curb and re-connected the spark plug wire. Then I drove downtown and parked on a parking lot near the Hotel Beaumont.

It was now only mid-afternoon, and I knew Mavis couldn't have arrived yet. By the time she got to downtown Houston, rented a car and fought city traffic coming back, she would be at least an hour and half behind us. I left word at the hotel desk that when a Miss Arlene Drake checked in, to please tell her to come to the bar. Then I sat in the bar and waited.

Mavis came into the cocktail lounge at 4:30 P.M. Her face looked strained, as though she had done a lot of worrying during the drive from Houston. She looked as though she needed a drink. I ordered her one and lit a cigarette for her.

She drained half of her drink in one gulp. It seemed to pull her together a little. "Where did you leave her?" she asked.

"In a motel," I said. "She thinks I'm having a fuel pump replaced. Did you register?"

She nodded. "I had a bellhop take my bag up, and came straight in here when they gave me your message. I haven't seen my room yet. But it's 325."

"Finish your drink and we'll go up to your room to talk," I told her.

Ten minutes later we were alone in her room. Ordinarily, even after so short a separation, Mavis would have moved into my arms for a kiss of hello the instant the door closed. Today she walked straight to the bed and seated herself on its edge as though her legs wouldn't support her any longer. Her gaze fixed on my face.

"You look ready to jump out of your skin," I said. "Don't you want to go through with this?"

A little unsteadily she said, "Yes, I want to go through with it."

"You sure you can? I don't want you coming apart at the seams on me."

"I'll be all right," she said. "I won't come apart at the seams. What's the plan?"

I examined her dubiously, wondering how well she would stand up under police examination, if it ever came to that. I said, "It has to look like an accident. The simplest thing would be to rig an automobile accident. Nobody's likely to question a highway accident. They happen all the time."

"Rig it how?"

"Have the car go over a steep bank somewhere. We can make it look as though I was thrown clear and Hannah was killed."

Mavis looked at me with such an odd expression on her face, I asked, "What's the matter?"

She said, "You haven't planned this out very carefully yet, Sam. It isn't like you."

"What do you mean?"

"Where do you find a steep bank alongside the highway around here? It's all flat country."

I felt myself grow a little red. What she said was true.

Apparently the idea of murder had such a paralyzing effect on me, my mental processes weren't working properly. My planning was panicky instead of cool and dispassionate as it usually was when I was setting up a bunco dodge.

Running a distraught hand through my hair, I said, "We'd both better get our feet on the ground, or we'll botch this. Maybe we're not up to murder."

"We're up to it," Mavis said quietly. Realizing that I was as nervous as she was seemed to have a steadying effect on her. "Just start thinking, Sam. Approach it just as though it was only a bunco dodge. You're smart enough to think up something foolproof."

Her words calmed me down a little. I *was* smart enough, I told myself. The scores we had made in the ten months since we met proved it. It was merely a matter of carefully figuring every angle.

"Let's go for a reconnaissance ride," I suggested. "We'll look for the right spot and plan what kind of accident to have according to the spot."

We took the car Mavis had rented, a new Ford sedan. I had her drive in the direction of the Louisiana state line.

As Mavis had suggested, there weren't any steep banks lining the highway in this section. But cutting the road there was an occasional gully that had to be spanned by a bridge. We stopped to examine two which were mere depressions a few feet deep, and where the road was as straight as a string. Neither seemed likely places for a fatal accident.

The state line is only a few miles from Beaumont. We found what we wanted just beyond it.

The gully was perhaps fifteen feet deep and a dozen

wide, with nearly-horizontal banks. The road curved to the left just before the bridge—a gentle curve, but nevertheless a curve. The guard-rail, a wide metal strip attached to concrete posts, looked impossible to break through except at terrific speed, which is hardly feasible in a rigged accident unless the rigger is prepared to die too. But the approach to the bridge was guarded only by a series of slim steel reflector rods that could easily be pushed over by a car bumper. The ground alongside the road was flat and hard, though it looked a little bumpy. It would be possible to push down one of the reflector rods and drive right to the edge of the gully, then jump clear just as the car went over.

"It hardly looks like a dangerous spot," Mavis said critically.

"Any spot's dangerous when the driver goes to sleep at the wheel," I said. "That will be my story. We'll do it here."

"When?" she asked.

"Tonight, between two and three A.M. I'll get Hannah to bed by eight. There won't be any problem there. She's always willing to go to bed. About two in the morning I'll wake her up, tell her I can't sleep any more and suggest we might as well hit the road again and reach New Orleans for breakfast."

"What do I have to do?"

"Just wait about a hundred yards this side of the bridge until we get here. I'll park behind you."

Mavis's face looked a little pinched. "She'll still be alive then?"

"Of course," I said. "It can't be done until the last minute, just before the wreck. They can tell by an autopsy when somebody dies."

"I see," Mavis said.

She didn't inquire as to why her presence would be necessary at the scene. She must have known that it really wasn't, as I could easily have worked the plan without her assistance. She could have stayed in Houston. She seemed to know she was there primarily as moral support, because I couldn't bring myself to murder alone.

Neither of us mentioned this. We both acted as though her part in the plan were as important as mine.

CHAPTER VIII

I WAS GONE from the motel over three hours. It was six P.M. when I returned. Hannah seemed neither suspicious nor impatient when I got back, though.

She merely laid aside the magazine she was reading, smiled and asked, "Get it fixed, dear?"

"Yeah," I said. "It was the fuel pump, all right. Let's go find a place for dinner."

As I had told Mavis, I had no trouble getting Hannah to go to bed early. She seemed to think it was a natural suggestion on a honeymoon. We were in bed by seven-thirty, though it was some time after that before she was willing to go to sleep. Nevertheless, by eight-fifteen she was snoring lustily.

I had no desire to sleep, even if I could have. I lay next to her without moving as the hours ticked by, my body so tense it ached. Every so often I checked the luminous dial of my wristwatch. The hands seemed to creep forward at a fraction of their usual pace.

An eternity passed before my watch told me it was midnight. It seemed as long again before the hands showed one A.M. I had meant to let Hannah sleep until two, but at 1:45 I couldn't stand the wait any more. I switched on the bedlamp and shook her awake.

"What's the matter?" she inquired sleepily.

"I'm all slept out," I said. "It's only two A.M., but we've been in bed six-and-a-half hours. Let's get up and get on the road. We can make New Orleans for break-fast."

Hannah stretched and yawned. "All right, honey," she said agreeably.

Twenty minutes later we pulled away from the motel. I hoped Mavis would be in place in time, as we were a good quarter-hour ahead of the schedule I had set.

Apparently Mavis had allowed herself leeway. Our headlights picked up her car parked on the shoulder just where I had told her to be. The only other vehicle in sight at the moment was a semi-trailer coming toward us. I slowed until it zoomed past, then swung over on the shoulder to park a few yards behind the Ford.

"What's the matter?" Hannah asked. "More car trouble?"

"Feels like a flat," I said. "Take a look at the tires on your side while I check the others."

Opening her door, she climbed out. I climbed out the other side, reached onto the floor in back and drew out the jack handle I had previously laid there. I walked around the rear of the car to Hannah's side, holding the jack handle behind me.

It was a dark night, but I had left the dim lights on and Hannah was peering at the tires by their reflected glow.

"They look all right on this side," she announced. Straightening up, she cast a curious glance at the Ford a few yards ahead of us, parked with its lights out. "Maybe that's some more honeymooners," she speculated.

I moved a step closer to her.

Then I paused. In the distance headlights appeared.

They neared rapidly as the car zoomed toward us at high speed. I waited, my hand still behind my back.

Hannah turned to look at me just as the car drew abreast. In the sudden glare of light she saw the expression on my face.

"What's the matter, Sam?" she asked in an alarmed voice.

The car passed, plunging us into relative darkness again. I brought my hand from behind my back and swung the jack handle with all my force.

I don't think she even saw it coming. There was a dull, crunching sound and she dropped without a murmur.

Reaching through the front window, I switched off the dims. Still carrying the jack handle, I walked up to the car in front. Mavis's pale face peered from behind the wheel. I dropped the bloody jack handle on the Ford's rear floor.

"Get rid of that when you get back to Houston," I said. "Drop it in the canal."

She asked huskily, "Is it over?"

"Yeah," I said. "Get out and help me get her back in the car. We have to work fast."

Opening the door, she climbed out. Hannah's body was dead weight, but together we managed to lift her back to a seated position in the front seat of the Plymouth. Slamming the door, I went around to the driver's side and climbed under the wheel.

Two cars passed, one from either direction. I waited until their tail-lights were dim red spots in the distance. "Well, here goes," I said. "Better go back to your car."

As she headed back toward the Ford, I started the engine, switched on the headlights and pulled around her. There were no cars coming from either direction. Where the curve began just before the bridge, I slowed to five miles an hour and kept straight on instead of turning with the road. My front bumper mowed down a reflector rod as though it were a match stick. Unlatching the door on my side, I held onto the handle and steered with one hand. I increased the speed to fifteen, jolting across the rough terrain straight for the gully.

Within feet of its edge, I flung the door wide and hurled myself from the car in a flying dive. The car continued on, nosed over the bank and landed hood-first with a rending crash.

In the dark I misjudged my distance slightly. I landed on hands and knees on the very lip of the gully, one hand and one knee on solid ground, the other frantically scrabbling at air. After teetering for a moment, I lost my balance and rolled head-over-heels down the bank to stop with a jolt at the bottom.

Groggily, I climbed to my feet. I was scratched and bruised and covered with dirt, and both trouser legs were torn, but otherwise I seemed to be undamaged. Though unplanned, the roll down the side of the gully added a beautiful touch. It made me look much more like a man who had been thrown from a car during an accident.

The Plymouth rested at a sixty-degree angle, nose down. It was as completely wrecked as though it had run into a brick wall at high speed. The force of the fifteen-foot-fall had driven the engine clear back into the front seat. Every window was broken except the rear one, which had popped out in one piece and lay on the ground intact. A strong stench of gasoline filled the air.

Shaken from my fall, I instinctively reacted as though I had been in an unplanned accident. I reached in and switched off the ignition. Both headlights were smashed, of course, but the tail-lights still glowed and the dash-light was still on. By its light I could dimly make out Hannah's body, oddly distorted and tightly imprisoned by mangled steel.

I didn't examine her closely. I couldn't. I had an urge to get away from there. Scrambling up the steep bank, I staggered over to the Ford, which Mavis had pulled forward to the broken reflector rod.

"Are you all right?" she asked fearfully.

"Just shaken up," I said. "Get going. I'll be phoning you in the morning to report the tragedy, and you'd better be at the house. Don't forget to ditch that jack handle."

"I won't," she said.

She put the car into drive and made a U-turn to head back toward Houston.

The first two cars I tried to flag down whizzed by without slowing. The third was a state trooper's car. When I told the two officers in it that I'd had an accident and my wife was pinned in the car, they both hurried down into the gully.

After examining the wreck by flashlight, they decided it was both hopeless and useless to try to get Hannah out. It was going to take cutting torches. They reported the location of the wreck over their radio and sped me to the nearest town for medical attention.

There wasn't the slightest suspicion about the accident on the part of the local police. They accepted at face value my story that I wasn't sure what had happened, but I must have fallen asleep at the wheel. The tracks of the tires showing that I had plowed straight ahead instead of rounding the curve bore out my story. While it was apparent from the tracks that I hadn't been traveling very fast, it was assumed that my foot had relaxed on the accelerator when I fell asleep, and the car had continued to roll along at reduced speed. My own minor injuries tended to make the whole thing more convincing. The general attitude seemed to be that it was a miracle I wasn't killed too.

Later I didn't encounter any suspicion in Houston either, though I think there was some speculation about my motive in marrying Hannah. At the funeral I finally encountered the various employees of the gym, all of whom attended out of respect, and I could sense that they were sizing me up. Probably the consensus was that I had married Hannah for her money, but there was no indication that anyone suspected I had killed her in order to enjoy it by myself.

When after a decent interval I called on the young lawyer who had drawn up our wills, I sensed the same attitude in him. He seemed sincere enough in his expressions of sympathy, but I couldn't help feeling that in the back of his mind he was thinking that I had moved in on a good thing. I believe that if her death so soon after our marriage had come in any way except a car accident in which I also received minor injuries, he would have suspected foul play.

The very nature of the accident worked to my advantage. The tragedy of a bride dying on her honeymoon inclined people to sympathize with the surviving bridegroom, even though they suspected it hadn't been exactly a love match.

It was the insurance investigator who put my heart

71

in my throat. The company sent its own man to Louisiana to talk to the police there, and later he came to Houston to interview me. He must have reported no suspicious circumstances, because nothing came of his investigation. But the very fact that an investigation was made was unnerving. If the company had decided to probe into my background, it could have been disastrous. As Samuel Plainfield was a fictitious name, they would have found no record of him in any of the places I claimed to have been. Which probably would have spurred a full-scale police investigation.

Probably only the fact that it was a paid-up policy forestalled a more thorough investigaton. Although I was a brand-new beneficiary, the policy itself had been in effect twenty years and had a cash-surrender value nearly as great as its face value. As paying it off represented no great loss to the insurance company, they probably felt more than a cursory investigation would be an unnecessary expense.

I hadn't anticipated any insurance investigation at all, though, and it left a lasting impression. Ever afterward, I felt a healthy respect for insurance investigators and was extremely careful in my dealings with insurance companies.

Mavis and I lived quietly in the house for a month after the funeral. In due course the will was probated and everything was transferred into my name. I waited a week, then unobtrusively put both the house and the gym up for sale through a real estate agent, asking fifteen thousand for each. Two days later he phoned that he had a blanket offer of twenty-four thousand for both. I think his buyer was a front for the real estate man himself, and probably he later unloaded them at a sizeable profit, but I was eager to wind matters up and fade from town. I took the offer.

The insurance check arrived two days after we got the money for the house and gym. Meanwhile, the probate court had turned over the bonds and Hannah's checking account to me. I cashed the bonds and closed out the account.

On May first, just a few weeks short of a year since Mavis and I had met, we bought another car and left Houston with a stake of sixty-seven thousand dollars. Three thousand of it was the residue from previous scores. The rest was from Hannah.

Mavis sighed with relief as we crossed the city line out of Houston. "We really earned this one," she said. "I think I've aged ten years in the past month."

"You and me both," I told her. "Our luck held all along the way. I get goose bumps when I think of how many things could have gone wrong."

Mavis shivered. "I thought we were goners when that insurance man showed up."

"We might have been goners if I hadn't accidentally rolled into the gully," I said. "It would have looked suspicious as the devil if I'd come through that wreck without even getting my hair mussed. We banked too much on luck. But at least we learned. Next time there won't be any luck involved."

"Next time? Why don't we get out, Sam? We've got enough of a stake to start some legitimate business. Let's not just pitch it away on high living."

"We've got a new business," I said. "A safe, reliable, steady one."

"What?" she asked.

"Lonely-hearts," I said. "There must be thousands of

73

women like Hannah throughout the country. They advertise in dozens of magazines that accept lonely-heart ads. We'll build up a sucker list from the ads. And next time we start running short of money, we'll be all set to go. We'll be able to pick and choose from a whole list of prospects."

"You mean you plan to marry more women?" Mavis asked on a high note.

"Marry them and bury them. The way I've been working it out in my mind during the past month, it'll be the safest racket in the world. Far safer than bunco dodges like the POW gag. Because the marks won't be around to report to the police how they've been taken."

Mavis said in a horrified voice, "You want us to go into the full-time business of murder, Sam? I thought it would be just this one time, because it was a special situation. We'll get caught and be executed, Sam."

I shook my head. "We won't even be suspected, the way I plan to run it. Anyway, you don't have to get excited. We won't be going back to work for at least a year. Not with the stake we've got. How'd you like to make a European tour?"

CHAPTER IX

BECAUSE OF a bad run of luck at Monte Carlo, the money didn't last a year. We were back in the States and at work again in six months.

We had learned a lot from the Houston job. The most important thing we had learned was to lower our sights and never again try for such a big score. The more money people leave when they die, the more speculation there is about their heirs. It was safer to pull small jobs regularly than to try to clean up with only an occasional big one. We concentrated on marks whose passing would leave only the faintest ripple of public comment.

The Houston job also taught us never again to try to operate on the mark's home ground. In small towns, where we found safest to operate, the death of a newcomer excites not nearly as much interest as the death of a lifelong resident. So we avoided women with deep roots in their own communities. If they weren't willing to move off with me to some new town after marriage, we by-passed them.

In the beginning we made some mistakes, of course. There was one harrowing experience where a curious brother traced a mark to a cemetery in Bismarck, Indiana, demanded a police investigation and stirred up a lot of newspaper speculation. We were living in another state under new names when the story appeared over the wire services, but reading about it gave us a jolt. We had left Bismarck only twenty-four hours before the brother appeared.

The experience taught us another lesson: to avoid women with close family ties.

As time passed, our procedure smoothed out until it was flawless. Eventually we were regularly pulling three jobs a year without exciting the slightest suspicion from anyone. Through experience and planning, we had entirely eliminated the element of luck from the racket.

In the summer of 1959, five years and three months after our meeting at the Beverly-Wilshire, Mavis and I were working a job in the little town of Tuscola.

The woman this time was a forty-year-old spinster who had been raised on an Iowa farm. Before I uprooted her and took her to Tuscola, she had never been out of the state of Iowa.

Mavis and I were using the same plan which had become our pattern. Ostensibly my wife Hazel and I were negotiating to buy the hardware business of an elderly merchant named Tom Benjamin, who wanted to retire. Mavis, as usual, was living with us as my sister. We had rented a house and were studying the community to see how we'd like to live in it permanently before closing the deal. We had been in town six weeks, and I was supposed to give Benjamin my decision in two more days.

The old hardware merchant had been devoting considerable time to trying to sell me on the town as a nice place to live. He had introduced me to practically every local group. The evening that Hazel had her fatal accident, he had arranged to take me to a school board meeting.

Luckily the sky had been overcast all that day, and it was quite dark by eight o'clock. Too dark for any neighbors to see me carry my burden across the back yard.

Old Tom Benjamin honked his horn out front promptly at eight-thirty. We had the scene all set, the lights off in the front room and only the light from the hall casting a dim glow to the front door. There was just enough light for Benjamin to be able to make out that a woman was waving good-by to me from the doorway without his being able to see who the woman was.

"I ought to be back about ten, Hazel," I called back to Mavis in the doorway.

From his car old Tom Benjamin shouted, "How are you, Mrs. Henshaw?"

"Fine," Mavis called back in an excellent imitation of Hazel's voice. She waved to him, then called to me, "Mavis will be right out, Sam."

Instead of getting into the car, I leaned in the front window and said, "I told my sister we'd drop her at the railroad station on the way to the meeting. Is that all right?"

"Sure," the old hardware merchant said. "Where's Miss Henshaw going?"

"Up to Chicago to visit our folks for a few days."

Then Mavis was coming down the steps wearing a light coat and carrying a small suitcase.

She had switched off the hall light, and now she called back to the completely dark doorway, "See you Friday, Hazel."

At the railway station, she gave me a sisterly kiss on the cheek and made the same announcement again.

Tom Benjamin's invitation for me to sit in and observe a school board meeting worked right in with my plans. I couldn't have asked for a more reliable group of alibi witnesses.

77

The meeting was over by ten-fifteen, and Benjamin dropped me off in front of the house a quarter-hour later. At that time of night, the streets of Tuscola were deserted, but light still showed in most of the homes.

When I switched on the front room light, I called, "Hazel!" Just as though I expected her to answer.

Mavis would have thrown me a sardonic grin if she had been there to hear. My increasing carefulness over the years had become a source of amusement to her.

I didn't consider it over-carefulness. While Tom Benjamin had already driven off, and no one else was on the street to see me enter, how did I know but what some snoopy neighbor was peering into my front room from a darkened window at that moment? They couldn't have heard me call Hazel's name, of course, but anyone in the house could have. I didn't want to overlook even the remote chance that some neighbor might have knocked at the back door just as I came up the front walk and, getting no answer, had stepped into the kitchen.

Through repeated practice, I had trained myself to act perfectly natural in these situations, even when I was sure there was no audience. Now I put a faintly puzzled look on my face when my call brought nothing but silence, and began to look through the house. I covered the three downstairs rooms, letting my expression grow more puzzled all the time.

Then I mounted the stairs, glanced into both bedrooms and the bath, and came downstairs again. For a few moments I stood in the front room with the vaguely irked expression of a man who is more disappointed than worried at not finding his wife home when he expected her.

Finally I went out the back way, crossed the lawn to

78

the Erlings' and knocked at their back door. Ed Erling came to the door.

"Evening, Mr. Henshaw," he said with a note of surprise in his voice. "Come on in."

"No thanks," I said. "I'm just looking for my wife. She over here?"

He shook his head. "Haven't seen her."

"I guess she must be over at the Shermans'. She can't be far, because she left the back door unlocked."

"Oh, you been out?" he asked.

"Mr. Benjamin took me to the school board meeting and I just got home. Well, thanks, anyway. I'll get over to the Shermans'."

That was normal enough, I thought as I crossed my back yard again toward the house the other side of mine. When it came time for Ed Erling to remember how I had acted tonight, he'd certainly recall that there had been nothing in my manner to indicate I was making an attempt to cover up a guilty conscience. I hadn't tried to look worried or implant in his mind that I was afraid something had happened to Hazel. I had made it a simple inquiry such as any husband might make when he unexpectedly found out his wife had gone out.

I stayed close to the rear of my own house as I crossed the yard, so as not to tread on any of the tulipbeds Hazel had set out all over the yard. In the dark I passed within feet of the old dry cistern with the pile of new lumber next to it, but didn't even glance in that direction. It was so dark I couldn't have seen it anyway, though from the corner of my eye I could make out the dim outline of the lumber pile next to it.

Of course Hazel wasn't at the Shermans' either. This time I let myself look thoroughly puzzled.

"She can't have walked down to one of the stores, because even the drugstore closes at ten," I said. "Wonder where she went?"

"Did you have the car?" Mrs. Sherman asked.

"No. Mr. Benjamin drove me to the school board meeting and back. I haven't looked in the garage."

"Why don't you look?" George Sherman asked.

I peered out across the dark yard. "You have a flashlight you could loan me, Mr. Sherman? Hazel will skin me if I walk on one of her tulip beds."

"Sure," Sherman said.

While he was gone after the flashlight, Mrs. Sherman asked, "Isn't your sister home either, Mr. Henshaw?"

"Mavis left for Chicago earlier this evening to visit our folks," I said.

George Sherman came back with the flashlight and handed it to me. I wanted him to stroll over to the garage with me, but I couldn't just bluntly ask him to. The whole thing would seem more natural if he trailed along on his own hook.

One of the first things I'd learned about George Sherman when I'd rented the bungalow next door to him six weeks before was that he was an avid Cleveland fan. Now I used the knowledge as bait.

As I moved across the back porch, I said, "Cleveland dropped one yesterday, I noticed."

With Sherman this was enough to start an evening-long dissertation. On several occasions I had listened to him explain his favorite ball club's 1954 Series performance so convincingly, he nearly had me believing its four straight losses were entirely due to bad breaks instead of the Giants' superior playing. Now he followed me down the porch steps explaining the Cleveland misfortunes which had brought about yesterday's loss. When I switched on the flashlight to start across the back lawn, he continued to follow, still talking.

The night was so dark, we could see nothing either side of the flashlight beam. When we neared the small pile of new lumber next to the cistern, I interrupted his apologia.

Flicking the beam over the pile, I said, "I've got to get to work on that cistern cover tomorrow before some kid falls through those rotten boards."

Then I let the light play over the square wooden cover of the cistern.

"It was that triple of Los Angeles' in the fifth," Sherman resumed. "With a batting average of only a hundred seventeen, who'd ever expect—Hey, looks like somebody already fell through there."

I had moved the light away from the cistern after holding it only long enough to give him a good look. Now I swung it back again.

"Yeah," I said, walking toward the cover, whose rotten boards we could now see had given way in the center, leaving a gaping hole.

When I knelt at the edge of the hole and directed the light downward, George Sherman leaned over and peered into the deep pit also.

"My God!" he said. "There's somebody down there!"

No one in Tuscola was even faintly suspicious of Hazel's death. The primary reaction of everyone in town seemed to be sympathy for me at losing my bride after less than two months of marriage. If this was tempered by the thought that a skinny bride of nearly forty whose main attraction had been a rather vapid good nature

81

shouldn't be an irreparable loss to a tall and fairly good-looking man of thirty-five, it wasn't apparent.

Nevertheless, the police had to make a routine investigation because of the nature of the presumed accident. Chief Howard Stoyle handled it personally, having me stop by his office the next morning. I found Tom Benjamin there too.

After the usual sympathetic cliches everybody uses in such circumstances, the fat chief said, "This is routine, you understand, Mr. Henshaw, but I have to ask some questions about last night. Just to try to fix the time of death and so on. Now I understand you were away from home at a school board meeting when it happened."

"Yes," I said. "Mr. Benjamin took me. I've been trying to get acquainted with as many facets of the town as I could, and he thought I might like to see the board in action."

"Your wife was all right when you left?"

"She waved to me from the door. That was about eight-thirty. The meeting was scheduled for a quarter of nine."

I looked at Benjamin for confirmation, and the old hardware merchant said, "That's right. She was alive at eight-thirty. I yelled hello to her from the car and she called hello back."

"What time was the meeting over?" Chief Stoyle asked.

"About ten-fifteen," I said. "It must have been about ten-thirty when Mr. Benjamin dropped me in front of my house."

"That places it between eight-thirty and ten-thirty," the chief said thoughtfully. "Which conforms to the coroner's guess. It was eleven when he examined the body, and he placed the time of death as two to four hours earlier. Far as you know, was your wife alone all evening?"

"My sister took the evening train to Chicago last night," I explained. "Mr. Benjamin and I drove her to the station."

When Benjamin nodded agreement to this, Chief Stoyle said, "Then she won't be able to tell us anything. No point in talking to her."

"She'll be available if you want her," I said. "I wired her this morning asking her to come home at once. It's only about a four-hour train trip, so she should be in by evening."

"Fine. But I don't think I'll be wanting her."

I said, "I can't understand what Hazel was doing out there in the dark."

"She had her hat on," the chief said. "We figure she decided to run downtown for something at one of the stores and was heading for the garage. Instead of sticking to the walk, she took a catty-corner shortcut, just as you and George Sherman were doing when you found her."

"She should have taken a light," I said. Then I made a hopeless gesture. "The worst of it is, I intended to build a new cover for that thing today. I already had the lumber for it."

"Well, it was a terrible tragedy, Mr. Henshaw. Particularly since you were still practically newlyweds. But don't go blaming yourself. It was just an unforeseeable accident."

Unforeseeable. I wondered what the fat chief would say if I told him that the main feature which had attracted me to the house when I rented it was the abandoned cistern with its dangerous-looking wooden cover.

There wasn't any more to the investigation. Chief

83

Stoyle didn't even question Ed Erling in order to verify that I had been to his house looking for Hazel. He did ask George Sherman a question or two as co-discoverer of the body, but he didn't even bother with Mrs. Sherman.

Later Mavis was, as usual, amused at how many of my precautions had turned out to be unnecessary.

CHAPTER X

I MET MAVIS at the station when she came in from Chicago. We both kept our expressions appropriately sad, but when I gave her a brotherly kiss on the cheek for the benefit of station onlookers, deep in her green eyes I could detect the suppressed relief she always felt when we neared the end of a deal.

Even in her ordinary dress Mavis had never been a beautiful woman so much as a desirable one. Except for sensually full lips, her features were too thin for real beauty. Yet properly clothed in the extremely feminine clothes she loved, she could start any man's pulse hammering.

As she was now, though, no man would have looked at her twice. Her tailored suit gave her a neat appearance, but it effectively hid the soft lines of her body. The prim way in which her sleek black hair was drawn back tightly gave her face a thin, bony appearance entirely missing when she wore it loose. Her stiff walk, lacking even the slightest hip sway, plus a total absence of makeup, completed the illusion that she was an eminently respectable and uninteresting spinster.

I had trained her well. She was no longer the amateur thespian she had been when we met. Now, in any part I set for her, she could put on as convincing a performance as any top actress.

I knew she was dying to ask how things had gone so far, but all she said was, "I'm terribly sorry, Sam."

The loungers at the station, watching us, nodded sympathetically.

Mavis didn't even ask any questions when we got back to the house. Even in privacy I insisted on preserving appearances. Once during dinner she did look at me somewhat pleadingly, but when I merely said, "Later," she let it drop.

In a town of only three thousand, there isn't much choice of funeral homes. I wouldn't have picked Jackson's otherwise, because Lyman Jackson was as curious about other people's business as an old woman. But he happened to run the only funeral parlor in town.

After dinner I took Mavis with me when I went to keep my appointment with Jackson. The plump, benign-looking funeral director courteously showed us to chairs in his office and seated himself behind a discreetly expensive desk.

"I can't begin to express my sorrow for your tragic loss, Mr. Henshaw," he said unctuously, then turned grave eyes on Mavis. "I know your sister by sight, of course, but I don't believe we've ever been formally introduced."

"Oh," I said. "Sorry. My sister Mavis, Mr. Jackson."

"How do you do?" Mavis asked politely.

"A pleasure, Miss Henshaw." His attention reverted to me. "I think first we should discuss the date and time of the funeral. Later, if you feel up to it, I'll show you our casket display and we'll talk over the type of funeral you wish. Or, if you prefer, we'll postpone that business until tomorrow."

I said, "I'd rather get everything settled tonight. I'd like the funeral as soon as possible."

"Of course," Jackson said, benignly placing his palms together. "Let's see now. This is Wednesday and the paper publishes tomorrow. We can have the notice printed and schedule the funeral as early as Friday, if you wish. Unless you want to allow more time for out-of-town relatives to get here."

"My folks are too old to travel," I told him. "And Hazel didn't have any relatives. Make it Friday."

We completed arrangements within a half-hour, deciding on a three-hundred-and-fifty-dollar package funeral. Funeral arrangements were another thing I was always very careful about. In a small town too cheap a funeral risks local criticism. Too elaborate a one excites comment. I always tried to keep them at an anonymous in-between level which would create little stir and be quickly forgotten.

After our business was completed, we had to go through the trying ordeal of satisfying the undertaker's curiosity about our future plans.

"Will this affect your negotiations with Mr. Benjamin?" he asked me as he escorted us to the door.

I was tempted to make some noncommittal reply, but then it occurred to me there might be some advantage in making use of Jackson's tendency to gossip. When Mavis and I pulled up stakes and left Tuscola shortly after the funeral, it might create less comment if the town were prepared in advance.

I said, "I'm afraid I haven't much heart for going into the hardware business right now, Mr. Jackson. Actually I haven't given my plans for buying out Mr. Benjamin's store a thought since this happened. But offhand I doubt that Mr. Benjamin and I will come to terms now. Hazel and I planned on the store together, and I don't think I could face it alone."

"I'm sorry to hear that," the undertaker said. "Mr. Benjamin will be disappointed. Undoubtedly he'll be able to find another buyer, though, so it will only temporarily postpone his retirement. I hope the town isn't going to lose you, Mr. Henshaw."

"I hadn't thought of that yet, either. But I wouldn't be surprised. It was only Mr. Benjamin's magazine ad which brought Hazel and me here in the first place. If I'm not going into business here, there won't be anything to hold me."

"Except sorrowful memories," Jackson agreed. "And I suppose it's wisest to flee those when you have no other roots. The town will be sorry to lose you, Mr. Henshaw, but I can't say I blame you for wanting to leave a community which has brought you such sorrow."

I hoped his feeling would be reflected by the rest of the community. The biggest single factor in our success was that we always managed to leave behind us a feeling of liking and respect and sympathy whenever we finally departed from a community. In the early days we had often left suspicion behind instead. A good deal of my careful planning was designed merely to leave pleasant memories of us in the townspeople's minds. Pleasant memories eventually fade and die, whereas suspicion has an unsettling habit of getting into the newspapers and warning future marks.

We finally broke away from Lyman Jackson. Mavis and I didn't speak until we were safely home and I had checked the house to make sure it was empty, locked the doors and drawn the Venetian blinds. This was safe now though I had refused to allow it before Hazel's death. The neighbors would expect to see drawn blinds at a home which had just suffered a tragedy.

When we were seated in the front room with drinks, I said, "Okay, you can relax now."

Mavis let out a deep breath. "Any sign of suspicion?" she asked.

I shook my head. "Chief Stoyle made a routine investigation, but everything was friendly and sympathetic. He doesn't even want to talk to you. The ticklish part is yet to come, though."

"You mean the bank and the insurance company? Why should it be ticklish?"

"I'm not worried about the bank," I said. "Soon as probate court gives the green light, I can withdraw the ten thousand in Hazel's and my joint account, and the bank won't have the right even to question it. But ever since Houston, insurance adjusters have always made me nervous."

"They've never yet fussed over the piddling little policies you insist on," Mavis said. "Five thousand dollars, when we could have cleaned up. We should have done what I wanted and insured her for ten thousand with a double-indemnity clause."

"Sure," I said. "If I listened to your advice, we'd be in jail long ago. Can't I get it through your head that insurance companies are *always* automatically suspicious of accidental deaths when there's a double-indemnity clause? The only safe policy to fool with is straight life, and even then it's dangerous to get greedy."

"But for fifteen thousand more," Mavis said wistfully.

"And fifteen times the risk. Remember that insurance

investigator in Houston? If they'd check on a policy that's been in effect twenty years, what do you think they'd do about one that's been in effect only two months? They'd want to look into my background clear back to birth. And when they found out Sam Henshaw didn't have any background farther back than two months, we'd be in real trouble."

"I suppose so," Mavis said reluctantly.

"Five thousand is about the limit any company will pay off on a new policy without suspicion," I told her. "We've got the five thousand Hazel put up to match mine in the bank account, plus five thousand insurance. What more do you want for two months' work?"

"Nothing, I guess. I know you've got more brains than I have, Sam. But we used to make such *big* scores. Sometimes for only two weeks' work."

"We used to be constantly one jump ahead of the police too, if you'll remember," I growled at her. "Now nobody ever gives us a suspicious look."

Until we turned out the lights and went to bed, we continued to follow my strict rule of keeping in character even when we were sure no one was watching. We had kept our conversation low enough so that no one could have heard it even by listening at a window, and nothing in our actions indicated that we were anything but a brother and sister having a nightcap together before we went to bed. In spite of Mavis's amusement at what she regarded as my overcarefulness, I didn't believe in risking even the remote chance that a peeping Tom might peer through the slats of a Venetian blind just at the wrong moment.

On the second floor of a darkened house, even I agreed that such precautions weren't necessary, however.

Ten minutes after I turned out my light and climbed into bed, the white figure I expected appeared in my bedroom doorway. As she padded toward me on naked feet, the glow of a nearby street lamp which cast its subdued light through the window bathed her in a soft glow.

She had loosened her dark hair so that it tumbled inky-black against the white of her bare shoulders. Her body moved with its natural animal sway instead of with the sedate stiffness she had assumed to go with her tailored clothes, and her full lips curved in a totally unsisterly smile.

As she came into my arms, she whispered, "It's been so long, Sam. Two full months of pretending to be your sister. And six weeks of lying awake nights thinking of you in here with Hazel."

"It was just as bad for me," I said in her ear. "How do you think I felt lying here next to a skinny bag of bones, when I knew my own lusciously-stacked legal wife was sleeping in the next room?"

"Am I lusciously stacked?" she wanted to know.

I didn't trust my memory. I started checking to make sure.

As Mavis had optimistically prophesied, we didn't encounter a bit of suspicion from any source. Tom Benjamin was disappointed that I wasn't going to buy out his hardware business after all, but he was understanding enough about it. He was an amiable old man, but a shrewd businessman nevertheless, and I think he had admired my caution in approaching the deal even though he was anxious to unload the store and retire. Putting off definitely committing myself until I had thoroughly

91

checked the business, and living in Tuscola long enough to make sure Hazel and I would like the place as a permanent residence impressed him only as sound business sense.

Now he accepted at face value my explanation that Tuscola could have only sad memories for me since my wife's death, and that I wanted to move back to Chicago.

Neither the bank nor the insurance company indicated any suspicion either. Within two weeks of Hazel's death, I got the insurance check in the mail. Meanwhile I had gotten a court order unfreezing Hazel's and my joint bank account. When I closed out the account, the only comment Bank President Smathers made was an expression of regret that the town was losing me.

Fifteen days after Hazel's funeral, Mavis and I drove out of town ten thousand dollars richer than we had entered it.

We still didn't entirely relax, though. I didn't believe in upsetting careful planning by getting careless at the last minute. We drove to Chicago, just as we had announced we intended to when we left Tuscola, and I sold the car. After that, if there were ever a belated attempt to track us from Tuscola, the trail would end at a used-car lot. That in itself wouldn't be suspicious, as there is nothing illegal about selling your car. It would merely prove that we'd returned to Chicago just as we said. But if anyone tried to trace us beyond the lot by attempting to locate the parents we were supposed to have in Chicago, he'd run into a dead end. Mavis and I had carefully avoided anything but the vaguest references to them, and an investigation of the Henshaws in the Chicago phone book would only turn up the information that none of them had ever heard of us.

A week after we left Tuscola we rented a small cottage at Miami Beach under the name of Mr. and Mrs. Sam Howard.

CHAPTER XI

During the next three months Mavis and I lived life as it should be lived. Daytimes we swam and fished or just lazed on our private beach until we were both brown as nuts. Evenings we toured Miami's night spots.

Once she dropped her spinster-sister role, Mavis was almost unrecognizable as the same woman. In evening gowns designed to accentuate her ripe figure instead of hide it as the rigidly-cut suits had, and with her coal-black hair hanging free instead of being pulled back in a tight bun, she caught every male eye whenever we entered a place.

In place of the staid and rather quiet spinster Tuscola had known, she became her true self. And her true self was a woman whose every movement and gesture was a proud flaunting of her sex.

Mavis had matured in five years. She was now thirty years old, and while she had changed little physically, she had undergone a profound psychological change. In place of the naïve young girl who had once picked me as a mark, there was a grown woman, with all the poise and self-confidence of mature experience. She had lost something in the process. The fresh air of innocence which had originally attracted me was gone forever. But she had gained something even more interesting to men in its place. She had become the embodiment of

94

sex. Her walk had the languorous motion of a sleepy cat; in her smile was enough promise to make even an octogenarian breathe heavily; and in her green eyes there was a constant invitation.

Mavis would have driven a jealous male crazy, for men had a way of looking at her with open hunger. Fortunately I wasn't a jealous man and, even after all these years, I was still unquestioned head of the family. She might flirt mildly with other men for the sake of gratifying her ego, but she wouldn't have dared to push it to the point of really making me jealous. She might also tease me a bit about unimportant things such as my elaborate carefulness, but she knew better than to belittle me in any way.

In some ways our relationship had an old-world flavor. Her role was to please her man, and deliberately making herself as alluringly feminine as she could was one of her marital responsibilities.

The careful habits I had developed in business had to some extent influenced our normal living habits too. When I wasn't playing the role of the lonely and frugal bachelor for the benefit of some equally lonely and frugal woman, I still tended to be pretty fast with a checkbook. But I wasn't the reckless spendthrift I had been in the early days. Perhaps this was partly because I was maturing too, and the pleasure I had once gotten from merely throwing money away had begun to wane. We still lived high, but where a few years ago we wouldn't have missed a night on the town until our money began to run short, we now often spent a quiet evening at home.

The result was that our money stretched much farther. Five years earlier we could have spent ten thousand dollars in six weeks. But our profit from the Tuscola job lasted three full months. Mavis gave me the news that our idyllic life was about to end one Friday afternoon. When I came in from a pre-cocktail swim, I found her pensively studying the bank statement which had come that morning.

"Do you know that we've gone through almost everything we made on the Tuscola job?" she greeted me.

I hadn't known, but it didn't particularly surprise me. Between jobs I let Mavis do all the worrying about our financial status, deliberately paying no attention to it myself. But I had been expecting the bad news at any time now.

I mixed a couple of drinks, handed Mavis one and spread my towel on the seat of one of the rattan chairs so that my swim trunks wouldn't get it wet.

"I suppose that means that it's back to work," I said. "Any prospects?"

During what you might call our vacations, it had become Mavis's job to line up potential clients. She did this by answering lonely-hearts advertisements in my name, whatever that happened to be at the moment, and building up a running correspondence with any women who sounded promising. Since I insisted on the women having rather strict attributes, sometimes it was rather difficult to locate just the right one. When she hit a snag, Mavis would run lonely-hearts advertisements in my name herself, which usually turned up somebody to satisfy my exacting requirements.

In line with my insistence on safety all along the way, the requirements I demanded were based on caution. The most important, a hangover from our close call in Bismarck, Indiana some years back, was that the woman have no near relatives she'd have to leave behind, so that the chance of anyone getting curious about her disappearance was lessened. If she had children or parents who lived with her and planned to continue making their home with her after she was married, it was acceptable. As long as whatever relatives she had were on the scene, they could be quietly disposed of between the time of the funeral and the time I collected, and a simple announcement that they'd gone back to their original home town would explain their sudden absence. It was surviving relatives, who didn't live with the mark, who might develop curiosity, that I tried to avoid.

Another thing I insisted on was that my potential wives didn't have too much money. Nobody is likely to pay much attention to the movements of a lonely spinster or widow who's worth only five or ten thousand dollars. But pick a woman in the hundred-thousand-dollar bracket, and her fellow townspeople are all going to be curious about who she's marrying, how she met the man, and where she intends to live.

The third attribute I insisted on was that she be at least fairly presentable, and not more than five years older than me. I didn't insist she be a raving beauty, because if she had been she wouldn't also be a lonely-heart, but I didn't want the citizens of whatever town we settled in to start wondering why a passably personable guy like me had ever married a revolting old bag.

Mavis took a sip of her drink before answering my question. Then she said in a wistful voice, "Sam, you know just a few years ago we once had nearly seventy-thousand dollars in our hands all at once?"

"Yeah," I said. "The first one. Hannah."

"Now we've got our five thousand bait money, plus about three thousand more. It doesn't sound like much progress."

"We've got five years of handsome living behind us."

Mavis took a deep breath and said rapidly, "Why don't we really do what you're always pretending to do when you line up a new wife, Sam? Use the eight thousand we have as a down payment on some small business."

"Oh, cut it out," I said irritably. "I don't want to listen to that crap again. We've got a safe racket that pays thirty thousand a year, tax free, for four to five months' work. I'm not breaking my back for peanuts in some two-bit retail store. What've you got in the way of prospects?"

With a little sigh she rose and went into the bedroom. She returned with the accordion folder in which she kept all her business correspondence.

"I had to run an ad this time," she said. "I couldn't find a single one to meet your lordship's tastes through the lonely-hearts clubs or by answering individual advertisements."

From the folder she drew a clipping of a small ad she had run in the personal column of a national confession magazine. It read:

Personable but lonely bachelor, age 35, with five-thousand-dollar bank account, desires correspondence with companionable spinster or widow of same age who possesses like amount. Object: parnership in small business and possible marriage. Samuel Howard, Miami Beach, Florida.

Grunting, I handed the clipping back to Mavis and she carefully filed it back in the folder.

"I got forty-seven answers," Mavis said. "Most of them from crackpots, as usual. Six sounded promising, but after a couple of exchanges of letters, I cut it down to two. I sent both of them your snapshot—that fuzzy one where you're far enough back so that it shows your handsome build and they can make out that you're not exactly repulsive, but your face isn't clear enough to be of much use as identification. Here's all the correspondence on them."

She handed me two piles of letters, about a dozen pieces in each. It took me twenty minutes to go through the lot, and meantime Mavis started dinner.

One of the women was a thirty-seven-year-old librarian in a small Arkansas town. She had five thousand dollars in the bank, she was a spinster and lived with her widowed mother. Her only other living relative was an uncle in Canada. Her photograph showed a plump, round-faced woman with a timid smile, who looked as though she probably didn't smoke, drink or use swear words stronger than Gosh.

The other was a thirty-two-year-old woman whose parents had died six months before and left the farm to her with the provision that she look after her younger brother. This wasn't much of a responsibility, she explained, as he was only ten years younger than she was, and perfectly capable of earning his own living. However, until he got married and set up his own home, he expected to make his home with her.

She said she had sold the farm for eight thousand dollars, five of which she was willing to invest in some suitable business if we managed to come to terms. Currently she and her brother were living in a rooming house in St. Joseph, Missouri. She had no other relatives, and added rather wistfully that she didn't even have any close friends. It seemed that during her folks' lifetime, both she and her younger brother had been too isolated by farm life to develop any friends.

The picture she sent was a miniature portrait photograph showing only her head and shoulders and giving no indication of what kind of figure she had. She had light hair, parted in the middle and hanging lifelessly on both sides of her face with no sign of wave in it. Her features were regular enough, but what looked like steel-rimmed glasses did nothing for them. Nevertheless, I judged that with a little help from Mavis she might be made passably presentable from the neck up.

I went back to her letters to see if I could get some idea of what her figure was like from a physical description I remembered seeing and skimming over. When I located it, I learned she was five-feet-four and weighed a hundred and fifteen pounds. At least she wasn't fat.

She also said her hair was ash blonde and her eyes gray, then added the interesting information that she still had all of her own teeth. On second reading I discovered that the picture was three years old, but she assured me she hadn't changed appreciably in the interim.

Mavis called, "Dinner in ten minutes," and I put the letters aside to go shower and dress.

We stayed home that evening. After dinner Mavis and I sat on the cottage's screened porch and discussed business.

"I like the sound of this farm-bred woman best," I said. "What's her name again?"

"Helen Larson. A Swede, I guess."

"You been following the ads of small-town businesses up for sale?"

"Just the last couple of weeks. There isn't any point in keeping a record of old out-of-date ads for places which would probably be sold when we got around to inquiring about them. There's a small dairy in Benton, Illinois, with an asking price of thirty thousand, with a third down."

"Too close to Tuscola," I objected. "We'll stay away from that section of the country this trip."

"Well, there's a tavern for sale in Rome, New York."

I gave her a disgusted look. "Without me you'd last about five minutes in this business. A tavern means a liquor license, and the New York State ABC board checks license applicants clear back to their birth."

"You wouldn't have to apply for the license until after you bought the place," Mavis said defensively. "And since you'd never actually buy it—"

I cut her off by asking, "What else?"

"A farm appliance store in Westfield, New York. That's way over in the west end of the state. Twenty-five thousand cash."

"That's our baby," I said. "Where's the ad?"

The ad had been cut from the current issue of a national farm journal, Mavis told me. It read:

For sale: Established farm appliance store with equipment and inventory worth fifteen thousand dollars wholesale. Five-thousand-dollar annual net earning. Price $25,000 cash.

The advertiser was a man named Herman Gwynn with a Main Street address in Westfield.

"A farm appliance store ought to appeal to a gal who was raised on a farm," I said. "Take a couple of letters."

CHAPTER XII

WHILE I always let Mavis handle the correspondence with women without paying much attention to what she was writing, she didn't know enough about business matters to handle that end. I had to do this myself.

The first letter I dictated was to Herman Gwynn, merely expressed interest in his ad and asked for further details. The second was to the Westfield, New York Chamber of Commerce. It went:

Gentlemen:

I have had considerable experience in retail merchandising and have been looking around for a chance to invest in a business for myself. I have answered an ad by a Mr. Herman Gwynn of your city who wants to sell his farm appliance business. The asking price is $25,000.

I have ten thousand cash to invest and would plan on financing the balance through one of your local banks if Mr. Gwynn and I come to an agreement. But before going to the trouble of a fifteen-hundred-mile trip, I would like certain information.

First, I would appreciate knowing if Mr. Gwynn is a member of your Chamber, as I would accept this as at least tentative evidence that he is a reliable businessman. Second, I would like your opinion on what my reception would be at your local banks if I wanted to take a fifteen-thousand-dollar mortgage on the business. And third, I would appreciate whatever general data you have available on the farm appliance business in that area, including the number and size of similar businesses I would be in competition with.

Very truly yours,
Samuel Howard.

"Now," I said to Mavis, "just exactly what have you written to this Helen Larson?"

Mavis's letters to the woman had followed their usual pattern. My wife wasn't very imaginative, which was the reason I could let her handle the love correspondence without supervision. She always told women approximately the same thing, varying only such items as place of birth and my work background to conform geographically to whatever part of the country we happened to live in at the moment.

This time she had me born on a farm in central Florida, as usual gave me only a high school diploma and had me the hired manager of a beach concession which sold sports equipment in order to explain our exclusive address. I discovered I had confessed to a steady income of forty-eight hundred a year, out of which I had managed to save slightly more than a seven-thousand-dollar nest egg.

Mavis had mentioned herself as my younger sister who lived with me and held a minor stenographic position. And as usual she had carefully inserted the information that I expected my sister to continue to live with me in the event I married.

Aside from that, the only real information she had

given out was that we had no relatives, having decided to dispense with a pair of aged parents on this trip. She had been purposely vague concerning the business-partnership angle mentioned in my ad, merely saying that I was investigating several alternatives.

When Mavis finished briefing me on what had passed between me and Helen Larson, I got out the Atlas and located St. Joseph, Missouri.

"About fifty miles from Kansas City," I said after studying the map for a few moments. "If she doesn't know anybody, that ought to be far enough away to meet her. Write her a letter and mention that I plan to be in K. C. soon. Don't pin it down to a definite date, but ask if she'd be interested in meeting me and talking things over in person."

"All right," Mavis said.

She got out her portable typewriter, and for the rest of the evening I watched television while she typed.

We got an answer from Herman Gwynn four days later, which led me to believe he was anxious to unload the store. In his letter Gwynn explained that his reason for wanting to sell out was that his wife's health required movement to a warmer and drier climate. He gave additional details about the business, including that the building was located on Main Street in the heart of Westfield's shopping district and that there were still six years to run on its ten-year lease, with an option to renew when the lease expired. He employed one male clerk and one female combination bookkeeper-clerk, both of which I could either keep or replace as I desired, as neither was under contract and could be discharged on fifteen days' notice.

Gwynn also enclosed a financial statement showing

that the business was unencumbered and that its net profit for the past two years had run $5,412.13 and $4,928.17 respectively.

Noting that the financial statement listed the book-keeper-clerk's salary as $2,500, it occurred to me that if Mavis and I hadn't been interested in the store merely as a decoy, it actually might make a pretty good legitimate business enterprise.

I said to Mavis, "I think we'd better sink our hooks into this thing fast before somebody really looking for a business makes him an offer. If Gwynn hasn't doctored his figures, a man and wife operating the place together and letting one employee go could net seventy-five hundred a year."

Just to satisfy my curiosity I got out a paper and pencil and figured out how long it would take to retire a fifteen-thousand-dollar mortgage at four percent interest if the principal was paid off at the rate of twenty-five hundred a year. It worked out to six years, with the first year's payment being thirty-one hundred and reducing at the rate of one hundred dollars a year, so that the final payment would be only twenty-six hundred.

Mavis had been watching me as I figured. I looked up at her and said, "If a couple with ten thousand dollars to put down could squeeze by on forty-four hundred the first year, and an increase of a hundred dollars a year for the next five years, they'd end up with a clear business bringing in about seventy-five hundred a year."

Her eyes turned bright. "Why don't we take it, Sam? I mean really."

I scowled at her and the brightness in her eyes faded. "In the first place we haven't got ten thousand dollars.

In the second place, I'm not sweating away six years of my life for the privilege of spending the rest of it in a one-horse town. Not while this racket continues to pay what it does."

"What good does it do us?" she asked quietly. "After five and a half years we've got two thousand dollars less than we had after pulling our first job together in Los Angeles."

I crumpled up the paper I had been figuring on and dropped it in an ashtray. "The good it does us is that we work less than six months a year, and not very hard even then. And live in luxury the rest of the time."

Mavis didn't say any more about it.

The reply from Helen Larson came the day after we heard from Herman Gwynn. She said she'd be delighted to meet me in Kansas City to talk things over, and wanted to know just when I planned to be there.

Three days afterward a letter came from the Westfield Chamber of Commerce which read:

Dear Mr. Howard:

I have your inquiry re: the Farmer's Appliance Store of Westfield, and glad to be able to report the following:

The present owner, Mr. Herman Gwynn, has been a resident of this village for forty years and we consider his character and business integrity beyond question. He has owned and operated the Farmer's Appliance Store for approximately twenty-five years and has been a member of this chamber for the same length of time.

As you probably know, the nature of the business is the retailing of all types of farm appliances except motorized equipment; i.e. it does not include heavy machinery such as tractors, harvesters and so on. But it offers for sale a variety of smaller farm equipment ranging from milking machines, pumps and cream separators all the way down to simple items such as buckets.

As Chautauqua County is one of the richest dairy and fruit sections in New York State, there is a steady market for this type of equipment. Nearly every city and town in the county contains at least one similar store, but there is no competition in Westfield itself, and the nearest competitor is in a town approximately eighteen miles away.

We do not have a locally-owned bank in Westfield. The only banking service is offered by a branch of the Chautauqua National Bank and Trust Company of Jamestown, New York. There is, however, a Westfield Savings and Loan Association.

I am sure that with ten thousand dollars in cash to invest, you would have no trouble raising an additional fifteen thousand from either institution, providing you can supply adequate character references and satisfy them as to your ability to run the business profitably.

I hope this information will be of service to you, and I will be looking forward to meeting you if you decide to become a member of this community.

Sincerely,
James Hope,
Secretary.

I put in a long-distance call to Herman Gwynn. When I got him on the phone, I said, "This is Sam

Howard, Mr. Gwynn. The man who wrote you about your store, you know. I'm phoning from Florida."

"Sure, sure," he said. "How are you, sir?" He had a rather pleasant voice, just beginning to turn high with age.

"Fine, Mr. Gwynn. I'm very interested in your proposition, and would like to come to Westfield to discuss it further. But I don't want to make that long a trip and have it turn out to be a wild goose chase. Is there any chance of your closing a deal with someone else within the next couple of weeks?"

"Well, a couple of other fellows have inquired about it," he said cautiously. "I couldn't rightly guarantee not to sell out if I got the right offer."

"Naturally not," I said. "That's why I called. To make you an offer which will protect us both. I'm willing to send you a check for two hundred dollars as a guarantee of good faith providing you'll guarantee me first crack at the store. The agreement won't bind either of us to any particular price, but will merely give me the privilege of meeting any offer you get from any other source before you close the deal."

He thought this over a minute before he said slowly, "How soon you planning to come up here, Mr. Howard?"

"I can't make it in less than about two weeks."

"That's hardly no time at all," he said. "You don't need to send any check, Mr. Howard. You sound like an honest man to me. And in these parts a man's word is as good as his signature. I won't guarantee not to bargain with no one else, but I'm willing to guarantee not to close any deal within the next two weeks, so you can get up here, look the business over and make an offer."

109

"Fine," I said. "You sound to me like an honest man too."

He asked me to let him know when I expected to arrive, and he'd meet me at the railroad station.

I said, "I may arrive by car. And I'm not sure, but I may be on my honeymoon. I'll phone you when I get there."

He sounded pleased that I was getting married. "I'll look forward to meeting you and your bride then," he said.

All that was left then was to check train schedules and wire Helen Larson the date I expected to arrive in Kansas City. It was then Friday, the thirteenth of November, and I actually planned to arrive in K.C. on the seventeenth. But I gave myself a day's leeway and asked her to meet me at the Croissant Hotel on Wednesday, the eighteenth.

When Mavis and I took the train from Miami we were still the rich and well-dressed Howards. We didn't change clothes and character until we got to Memphis, which was at the end of our train ride.

In Memphis we put into storage all of my tailored clothes and Mavis's evening gowns, expensive dresses and furs. I switched to the good grade but slightly ill-fitting suit which made me look like an honest but not-too-well-off clerk of some kind. Mavis returned to her staid ready-made suits, her prim hairdo and the sedate manner of an inhibited spinster.

I bought a secondhand Ford in Memphis and drove the last four hundred and seventy miles.

Mavis and I checked into adjoining rooms at the Croissant at six P.M. on November seventeenth. The Croissant was a good second-class hotel, fully respectable enough to match our supposed middle-class respectability, yet with rates within the means of the frugal characters we were supposed to be.

That night when Mavis slipped into my room through the connecting bath and crept into my arms, she said, "Oh, Sam. I can't bear to think of the next two months, watching you with another woman again. Couldn't we at least talk to this Gwynn man with the eight thousand we have?"

"No," I said. "And I don't want to hear you mention it again."

CHAPTER XIII

THE DESK PHONED at eleven-thirty the next morning to tell me I had visitors in the lobby. Mavis and I had been up and dressed since eight, but had stuck to our room awaiting the call, even having breakfast sent up so that we'd be sure not to miss the Larson woman when she arrived.

I said into the phone, "Tell them to wait and I'll be right down."

"Them?" Mavis asked when I hung up.

"She must have brought her kid brother along," I said. "Glad she did. It'll give us a chance to size him up. You ready?"

Mavis checked her reflection in the mirror a final time to make sure that she was. Watching her, I thought it was amazing how much difference clothes and hairdo and manner could make in her appearance. More than actual beauty it was Mavis's mobility and the aura of sexiness about her which made her such a desirable woman. With her normally flowing movements restrained to a kind of stiff primness, half of the impact she had on males was destroyed. And no woman could have looked sexy in the severely-tailored suit she wore, which made her look flat-chested and hipless.

As we went down the stairs, I couldn't help feeling proud of the excellent job of training I had done on Mavis.

There were several people in the lobby, but we didn't have any trouble picking out Helen Larson and her brother. They were seated side-by-side on a sofa facing the stairs, self-consciously trying to appear at ease.

As we reached the bottom of the stairs, the woman glanced at me without recognition, which wasn't surprising in view of the fuzzy picture Mavis had mailed her.

I had no trouble identifying her, though. As she had written, she had changed very little in the three years since the picture she sent had been taken, the only difference being that her hair was now drawn straight back and clasped at the base of her neck by a metal circlet instead of being allowed to hang on both sides of her face. And that was no improvement.

She wore a cheap and shapeless wool dress cut like a sack, which made it impossible to judge what kind of figure she had, except that it was on the slim side. But there was some promise in the visible portion of her legs. Despite gray cotton stockings and low-heeled shoes, I could see that her calves were nicely rounded and her ankles pleasantly slim.

As indicated in her photograph, I saw that her features were regular enough. But her steel-rimmed glasses plus an innately corn-fed appearance spoiled the effect of whatever natural attributes she had.

Her most attractive quality at first sight was cleanliness. She was scrubbed so thoroughly, she literally shined. For a startled instant I thought I recognized in her a resemblance to Hannah Stokes, my first lonely-hearts bride. Then I realized it was only her freshly-scrubbed appearance, which Hannah had possessed too, and that there was no physical similarity between the two women at all.

Before crossing over to the sofa, I paused to study the brother, too. He wasn't an unhandsome lad in an awkward and farmer-like sort of way, I noted. He was lean and big-boned and had large-knuckled hands which he didn't seem to know what to do with. He looked Swedish, mostly because of blond hair the same color as his sister's. His hair needed cutting so badly, it hung over his tight collar at the back.

The thing I liked best about him was the utter stupidity on his face. It had occurred to me that a twenty-two-year-old boy might be mature enough to be wary about his sister getting involved with a complete stranger. But after one look at this lad, I knew there was little danger of his creating an awkward situation.

I suspected that what the woman had written about his being able to support himself was merely hopefulness, because he didn't impress me as having sense enough to come in out of the rain.

When I had completed my study, I touched Mavis's arm and we continued on across the lobby. Stopping before the couch, I said in a polite voice, "Miss Larson?"

The woman looked almost frightened. Then she blushed scarlet and jumped to her feet. When her brother rose more slowly, instead of looking at me her eyes sought his face in a plea for moral support.

I was used to this reaction. Like all the others in the past five years, she had probably never before even been looked at by a man. And now, meeting for the first time the man she had been dreaming might become her husband if arrangements worked out to our mutual satisfaction, her tongue simply deserted her.

She was probably also a little flabbergasted by my appearance. Though nearing thirty-six now, I didn't look much different than I had when Mavis and I first met. Much swimming during our frequent vacations had kept me lean and hard, and at the moment I was deeply tanned from the Florida sun we had just left. Also Mavis had often told me I have an air of virility about me which appeals to women. Once when I tried to pin her down as to exactly what she meant by that, she explained it by saying, "You just look like you'd be pretty terrific in bed." Then she had generously added, "Which you are, as it happens."

I don't suppose the woman had expected to meet a matinee idol through a lonely-hearts ad, but I was probably better looking than she had expected.

I said in a kindly voice, "I'm Sam Howard and this is my sister Mavis." I thrust out a hand at the young man. "You must be Helen's brother."

Reaching out gingerly, he gave my hand a jerky shake. "Yeah."

He nodded shyly at Mavis, then looked at his shoes.

Mavis greeted them both politely and Helen said something in a barely audible voice which I took to be acknowledgement of the introductions.

I said to the young man, "Helen never mentioned your name in her letters."

"Huh?" he said, looking up briefly. "Oh. It's Dewey. Dewey Larson." His feet shuffled in embarrassment and his gaze dropped to them again.

"It's nice to meet you in person finally," I said to Helen.

Her blush had faded, but now she flamed red again.

She cast a covert side glance at her brother and didn't say anything.

"I don't suppose you've had lunch, have you?" I asked.

This time she looked at me and managed a faint, "No, sir."

I grinned at her. "You make me feel like a grandfather. Let's start out on an informal basis right from the start. You call me and my sister Sam and Mavis, and we'll call you Helen and Dewey. Okay?"

She smiled shyly. "All right, Mr.—" She paused, looked stricken and hurriedly amended it to, "All right—Sam."

"Suppose we get acquainted by having lunch together here in the hotel restaurant? It's a little early, but there'll be less of a crowd now."

Helen agreed for both herself and her brother, who seemed incapable of speech except in answer to direct questions.

During lunch I made no attempt to discuss either our possible business partnership or our possible marriage, preferring merely to size Helen and her brother up and at the same time put them at ease so that they could form some opinion of us.

Gradually both thawed out when they discovered conversation was going to stay on a small-talk level. When the coffee arrived, they were still hardly vivacious luncheon companions, but at least Dewey had stopped looking at his feet, and Helen no longer blushed every time I spoke to her.

I discovered to my pleasant surprise that the woman wasn't unintelligent in a quiet sort of way. She wasn't completely uneducated either, apparently having read a surprising number of books, though she confessed to

116

an almost total lack of formal education. I guessed that books had been her substitute for social life, for she seemed woefully ignorant of any actual experience outside of what had occurred to her on the farm.

Even after he lost his initial embarrassment, Dewey confirmed my first opinion of him. He not only possessed no more worldly experience than his sister, he seemed to have read nothing in his life but comic books and pulp magazines. Mentally, he seemed to be still in his teens.

I decided that if Dewey were capable of earning his own living, as Helen had suggested in her letters, it would have to be by some manual endeavor. Probably he could make a go at farm labor, since he'd been raised on a farm, but I doubted that he'd even make a howling success at that. He had the physique for it, though, even if he did lack the brains. He exuded the rugged good health of outdoor living, his youthful face still showing sun wrinkle about the eyes even after six months off the farm.

When the check came, Helen started to fumble at her cheap cloth purse. I smiled at her.

"I invited you and your brother to lunch, Helen."

She stopped fumbling and looked at me, her eyes wide behind their glasses. Then she smiled back.

I guessed it was probably the first time in her life a man had ever taken her to lunch.

As we all moved back toward the lobby, I said, "Now that we're all acquainted, suppose all four of us go up to my room and discuss what we want to come of this meeting."

For the first time since she had begun to relax, Helen

blushed again. But she said in a steady enough voice, "All right, Sam."

There were only two chairs in my room. I let Helen have the easy chair, Mavis the straight one and I told Dewey to sit on the bed. I remained standing myself.

I started out by saying, "Helen, we both know that at least half the reason for this meeting is that we're both lonely people and we hoped we'd find in the other a suitable spouse. I don't know what your opinion of me is, but you're everything I expected to find and a little more."

"Oh, I think you're very nice," she blurted, then blushed furiously.

I said, "Even though we liked each other right off, I'm sure neither of us wants to decide on the basis of such a short look. You planning on staying over here tonight?"

Helen said, "Well, I don't know. We didn't really make any plans. I mean—" She trailed off and looked at her brother, who merely gazed back at her vacantly.

"Why don't you let me see if I can get you and Dewey rooms here at the hotel?" I suggested. "Then we can spend all afternoon and this evening getting acquainted. Meanwhile, we'll just table marriage talk until morning."

"All right," Helen said. She seemed both relieved at the postponement and slightly disappointed at the same time.

Picking up the phone, I got the desk and discovered that there was a pair of connecting rooms available right across the hall from Mavis's and mine. I told the clerk to hold them for a Mr. Dewey Larson and a Miss Helen Larson, who'd be down to register for them later.

When I hung up, I said, "While we're getting acquainted, there isn't any reason I can't explain the business partnership end of this thing, in case we decide to get together. I've been checking a number of small businesses recently. In fact one was in Independence, only a few miles from here, which is what brought me and my sister up this way. It petered out, though. The best prospect seems to be a farm appliance store up in Westfield, New York."

Helen said, "Farm appliances. Oh, I'd like that. I know something about them."

Opening my suitcase, I got out the correspondence concerning the business and showed it to Helen. She read it all carefully, paying particular attention to the financial statement Herman Gwynn had sent. When she got to the copy of my letter to the Westfield Chamber of Commerce and its reply, she looked up at me with an expression of startled respect.

"I would never have thought of writing to the Chamber of Commerce," she said. "You really know a lot about business things, don't you?"

Mavis said primly, "Sam will make an excellent businessman. He should have been in business for himself long ago, but he's never had the stake to get started."

"Here's the way I figure it if we do manage to take over the business," I said. "If we both work in the store, we can let the bookkeeper-clerk go and boost our net income to seventy-five hundred a year."

In detail I went over the same figures I had explained to Mavis. When I finished, I could see that Helen was already sold.

"How about Dewey?" she asked. "Could he take the place of the clerk they have now?"

I glanced at Dewey, who sat with his large-knuckled

hands dangling between his knees, looking like a handsome version of Mortimer Snerd. If I'd actually planned to invest in a business, I wouldn't have hired him to sweep the place out. But since I had no intention of finally closing the deal, a promise was easy.

"Sure," I said. "According to the financial report, the male clerk gets two thousand and eighty dollars a year, which comes to forty dollars a week. Dewey might as well get it, and we'd still have the same net profit. He'd just be on salary, though. It isn't a large enough business for more than two partners."

"Oh, Dewey wouldn't expect an interest in the business," Helen assured me. "The folks left the farm just to me anyway, so the money from its sale is all in my name." She glanced at Mavis timidly, "How about your sister?"

"I'll get some kind of stenography job," Mavis said. "Don't worry about me being a burden on you. I've always paid my share of the expenses with Sam."

Helen blushed. "I didn't mean that," she said flusteredly. "I mean, it hardly seems fair putting my brother in the store and leaving you out."

"I wouldn't clerk in a store where you have to stand on your feet all day for half-interest in the business. I'll get a job, all right."

CHAPTER XIV

HELEN seemed relieved that this problem was settled. She turned back to me. "If we decide to—to come to an agreement, Sam, how will we work it about the money? I mean the five thousand we each put up?"

"I've actually got about eight thousand," I said. "A little less since I bought a car. And I understand from your letters that you've got about the same amount. What I planned in case we do decide to get married was to move up to Westfield and rent a house for the four of us. I'd want to take about six weeks to study the business and get acquainted with the community, so we'd be sure we liked living there, before I closed the deal. But we can't just string this Gwynn man along for six weeks without showing some evidence that we're at least capable of buying him out if we decide we want to. We'd each deposit five thousand in a joint savings account at the local bank. With that as evidence of our financial position, I can arrange with the bank for the fifteen-thousand balance we'll need as a mortgage loan, without actually signing anything until we definitely decide. But once even oral arrangements are made, I can ask the bank to inform Gwynn that we're in a financial position to close the deal."

"What's a joint account?" Helen asked. "I don't know much about business."

"One in both our names. The pass book would be

made out to 'Samuel Howard or Mrs. Helen Howard.' "

Her cheeks reddened a little at the "Mrs. Helen Howard."

"Then it would take both our signatures to draw it out?" she asked.

"No. Either one of us could. We could have an account requiring both signatures by making it read 'Samuel Howard *and* Mrs. Helen Howard' instead of *or*, but it wouldn't be very smart. If I happened to die suddenly, the whole account would be frozen until the estate was settled. This way it'd be frozen for a time anyway, but only until you could get a court order authorizing you to draw on it."

I didn't point out that if she happened to die suddenly, the same situation would obtain.

She said, "If we do get—if we decide to get married, what would you want me to do? About my money, I mean. If we're going clear off to New York State, I couldn't leave my money in the bank here. But I wouldn't want to carry that much around in cash."

"Naturally not. What bank's your money in?"

"One in St. Joseph."

"Well, when you draw it out—" I paused to grin at her. "Or, rather, *if* you draw it out, ask for the whole thing in a single bank draft. I have a bank draft for seven thousand, plus enough in traveler's checks to get us married and up to Westfield. When we get there we'll each put five thousand in a joint savings account and the balance in a joint checking account."

"That sounds all right," she said in a relieved tone. "I'm ashamed of myself for knowing so little about business and financial things. I'm afraid I'll have to depend on you to tell me what to do all along the way."

That suited me fine.

We dropped the subject of business then, and spent the rest of the afternoon and that evening getting acquainted. On my suggestion that Helen and I could get to know each other better if we spent some time alone, we left Mavis in Dewey's company and went off together.

It was a brisk but sunny day, and for most of the afternoon we just drove around and talked. As time passed I found the woman a more and more pleasant companion. Once her initial shyness had completely worn off, I discovered she could converse quite freely within her limited experience, and that she had a quiet but warm sense of humor.

She even became a little more attractive physically, though she hardly started my pulse fluttering. Seated in the car, the impossible dress she wore for some reason hung a little differently than when she was seated in a chair or standing. While it could hardly be described as clinging to her body even then, I could see that beneath her open coat it gave a faint impression of soft curves concealed under its looseness. If Mavis could manage to get her a dress designed to flatter whatever figure she had, she might look quite presentable.

Her hair was unusually soft and glossy, I noted also. A different hairdo might improve her a hundred percent. And once when she slipped off her glasses to clean the lenses, I was surprised to discover that her features in profile were really excellent. Her teeth were nice, too, small and even and white.

I started making mental notes of the changes I wanted Mavis gently to induce in order to make the woman look less like a fugitive from the back woods.

Mavis and Dewey weren't expecting us back before

ten o'clock. Helen and I had dinner at a downtown restaurant and afterward went to a picture show. When we finally got back to the hotel at ten, I knew it was in the bag. Helen's eyes were shining and she was chattering as freely as a debutante at her coming-out party.

She seemed a little amazed at herself at being able to get along with a man so unreservedly, but it didn't amaze me. Getting women to relax and learn to like me was my business.

I cinched it by leaning down and gently kissing her on the lips when I left her in front of her door. She blushed to the roots of her hair and stood there staring at me as though she didn't know what to do or say.

I took her key from her unresisting hand, unlocked the door, and handed the key back to her.

"Good night, Helen," I said, smiling at her. "See you in the morning."

She was still standing in the hall staring after me, a radiant expression on her face, when I keyed open my own door. Then she turned quickly and entered her room.

Mavis was still up and waiting for me to come in. She had left both doors of the connecting bath open, and the moment I entered my room, she appeared in the bathroom doorway. She merely looked at me inquiringly.

Locking the door to the hall, I said, "We're in. Right after breakfast tomorrow I'll drag her downtown for the license and blood tests. There's a three-day waiting period here, so we won't be able to get married until Sunday. Meantime I'll have her go back to St. Joseph, pack up her stuff, close out her bank account and come back here to wait it out."

"I suppose as usual I'll have to prod her into different

124

clothes and a beauty treatment," Mavis said without enthusiasm.

"You don't think I'd take her to Westfield as she is, do you? The whole town would figure it was a shotgun marriage. Tomorrow morning I'll manage to break her glasses accidentally. Naturally I'll insist on paying for new ones. You go along for the fitting and pick out better-looking frames. By Saturday they ought to be ready if you insist on quick service. The same day you pick them up, you can help her shop for a wedding outfit. I don't have to tell you what to buy. You've had enough experience."

"Yes," Mavis said. "I love making your women presentable so they won't be a public embarrassment to you."

She pushed the door shut with the barest suggestion of a slam and went back to her room.

But ten minutes later, after I was in bed, she returned dressed in the plain woolen wrap-around robe she had substituted for her usual filmy negligees when she assumed the role of my sister. By the way it hugged her body, I could tell she had nothing on under it. She stood in the bathroom doorway, her figure silhouetted by the light behind her, and simply waited.

"No," I said. "Not with them right across the hall."

"Both our doors are locked," Mavis said tonelessly.

"Sure. But on the off-chance that Helen decides on a midnight tête-à-tête, it would sound fine for her to hear you scrambling back to your own room when she knocked on the door, wouldn't it? Starting right now, you're my sister twenty-four hours a day, every day, until the deal's finished."

This time there was more than a mere suggestion of a slam when she closed the door.

Everything went off as I had scheduled it the next morning. At breakfast I told Helen frankly I thought we'd make a good marriage partnership. Helen blushed, looked at her brother for approval, and when he indicated interest in nothing but his eggs, admitted in a low voice that she thought so, too.

Mavis offered me congratulations and wished Helen happiness, both in a dry voice which irritated me, but whose tone seemed to be missed by Helen in her mixture of confusion and happiness. Dewey then came back to earth long enough to realize what was going on, seemed to think something was expected of him, and after thinking it over, tentatively offered me his hand.

I shook it heartily and said, "Thanks, Dewey. You can be best man, if you will. And Mavis maid of honor, if Helen wants her."

"Oh, I do," Helen cried.

Tenderly I looked into Helen's eyes, then gave a little chuckle. "Honey, your glasses are so dirty, I don't know how you see through them. Let me give them a wipe."

Reaching out with both hands, I lifted them from her face. Then, negligently holding them by one earpiece with my left hand, I whipped a handkerchief from my breast pocket with my right so enthusiastically, the end of the handkerchief swept the glasses from my loose grip and hurled them a dozen feet away. They landed on the asphalt-tile floor and shattered.

"I'm so sorry," I said contritely, pushing back from the table and going to recover the pieces.

Both lenses were broken and the frame was bent in two places.

126

When I returned to the table and handed the wreckage to Helen, I said in an embarrassed voice, "Looks like my first gift to you is going to be new glasses. We'll go downtown and get them this afternoon."

Mavis came through on cue. "I'll take her to an optician," she offered. "I can help her pick out the frames."

Helen insisted that the accident wasn't my fault and that she'd buy the new glasses herself.

"That'd be silly," I said. "What difference does it make who pays? Everything we have is going to be joint assets in a few days."

She admitted the logic of that. Then she said, "I'll have to be led around until the new glasses are ready. I run into things without them. And we can't possibly get married until then."

"Why not?" I asked.

She smiled at me shyly. "I'm so blind without glasses, I'm afraid I might marry the wrong man."

She may have been as nearsighted as she claimed, but it hadn't affected the appearance of her eyes. Without the glasses on I was startled to discover they had the depth and color of sapphires.

Spontaneously I said, "Why you have beautiful eyes, Helen."

Helen turned bright red. Her gaze darted in all directions in an attempt to cover her embarrassment at the unexpected compliment, which in all likelihood was the first bit of flattery she had ever heard from a man.

Mavis's lips thinned into a disapproving line. I gave her a sharp glance and she smoothed the expression away. With an effort to sound friendly, she said, "You do have pretty eyes, Helen. It's a shame you have to wear glasses."

The rest of the day Helen was kept fairly busy. After

breakfast I took her downtown, applied for a license and we had our blood tests. That took most of the morning. In the afternoon Mavis took her to an optician, where a long wait, the eye examination and the selection of frames used up most of the rest of the day.

Helen readily agreed to my suggestion that she return to St. Joseph only long enough to pack and close out her bank account. I decided to drive her up on Friday morning instead of sending her by bus, as it was only fifty-two miles. Dewey decided he'd go back too in order to pack his own stuff instead of making Helen do it, and as Mavis didn't care to be left all alone, in the end all four of us went.

I wasn't enthusiastic about being seen by anyone Helen and Dewey knew, but the risk wasn't too great. She and Dewey had no really close friends, and apparently not even many acquaintances aside from their landlady. Mavis and I avoided meeting the landlady by the simple expedient of waiting in the car while Helen and Dewey collected their things and said good-by to the woman.

They didn't seem to have many worldly possessions. Dewey lugged out only two large suitcases and one small one to load in the trunk.

Dewey, Mavis and I all waited in the car when Helen went into the bank to close out her account. When she came out, she proudly showed me the bank draft.

She had had it made out to Mrs. Helen Howard.

"How are you going to cash it if I leave you waiting at the altar?" I asked her teasingly.

Her face fell, and for a moment I thought she didn't know I was joking. Then she said timidly, "I really haven't the right to use the name yet, have I?" and I realized she was only concerned because I might think her too forward.

I said with a smile, "It'll be your legal name by the time you get around to cashing it in Westfield. I'm not going to leave you at the altar."

It amused me that she actually looked relieved.

CHAPTER XV

ON THE way back to Kansas City I casually delved into what Helen had told people in St. Joseph about her plans.

I learned she had told her landlady she was getting married and moving to New York State, but hadn't told her to whom, or where in New York State. She hadn't mentioned anything at all to anyone else.

That afternoon, while I lined up a justice of the peace who was willing to marry us on Sunday, Mavis took Helen shopping for her trousseau. Whatever they bought, they didn't bring it back to the hotel with them, for Helen returned wearing the same shapeless dress she'd had on when we met and had worn ever since. She seemed quite excited, however, though she refused any information aside from a mysterious reference to some alterations being made.

Saturday was the big day for Helen. She went off with Mavis right after breakfast, announcing that she wouldn't be back until five P.M. When I inquired what was going to take all day, Mavis explained that they had to pick up the new glasses, had several clothes fittings scheduled, and that Helen had a three-o'clock hairdressing appointment.

Helen was wide-eyed with excitement.

"I've never before been in a beauty shop," she confessed naïvely just before she and Mavis left.

My slightly ill-fitting suit having served its purpose of

not making me look too smooth to be believable, I got out the plain dark business suit I'd also brought along and sent it out to be pressed. It too was ready-made, but of good quality and fit. A slight increase in sleekness can be expected of a man on his wedding day.

Then I got a haircut, taking Dewey along with me in the hope that he'd do the same. He didn't take the hint, however, but sat and read comic books while he waited. When I stepped out of the chair, I decided to employ a frontal attack.

"Aren't you going to get your hair cut for the wedding?" I asked him.

"Huh?" he said.

Getting up, he looked in a mirror, seemed surprised at the length of his hair and climbed into the barber chair I had vacated without further comment.

I told the barber to cut it close.

The result was remarkable. With a decent haircut the boy would have been almost handsome except for the stupid look on his face.

Dewey had worn the same shiny blue serge suit he had on when we met ever since I had known him. It was much too tight and sadly in need of pressing. I asked him if he wanted to get it pressed before the wedding.

"I got another one up in my room that's already pressed," he said.

Nothing could turn him into a sleek and sophisticated best man, nor hide his farm upbringing, I realized. But seemingly he was at least going to make the attempt to be presentable.

My preparations for the wedding didn't take nearly as long as Helen's. I was all through by eleven o'clock in the morning. I spent a dreary day in Dewey's company.

I didn't know what Helen's habits were, but Mavis was always prompt. When she said they'd be back at five, I knew she meant right on the dot.

I decided to wait for them in the lobby.

Dewey had gone up to his room, finally, and left me to enjoy the lack of his company. At five I was waiting alone by the cigar counter, a spot which gave me a good view of both the front and side doors into the lobby. I'd been there about five minutes, glancing up each time either door opened, but it was always someone else coming in.

Exactly at five the revolving door at the side of the lobby spun, and I glanced that way expecting to see Helen and Mavis. But it was a woman alone, a slim and sleek blonde with an upsweep hairdo and harlequin glasses, dressed in a clinging white knit suit and a yellow three-quarter length coat which hung open to show the smooth lines of her body. Idly I admired her figure as she crossed the lobby, then my admiration turned to faint puzzlement.

Part of my puzzlement was due to the way she was teetering on her high heels, as though she found balance difficult and was in danger of turning an ankle at any moment. The rest was due to the fact that she was bearing directly at me.

When she got within five feet, my puzzlement turned to utter astonishment. The woman was Helen Larson, and she was very nearly a raving beauty.

Stopping directly in front of me, she smiled tentatively. I made no attempt to close my mouth as I slowly looked her over from head to foot.

132

Mavis's taste in clothes had always been excellent, but this time she had outdone herself. I had expected her to find Helen something which would compliment her figure. But the knit dress did more than just flatter it. Helen's figure didn't need flattery. The dress clung to her body, revealing everything the shapeless sack she had worn previously concealed.

The concealment had been a crime.

High-heeled shoes rounded out calves as perfect as a Varga girl's, and they were encased in sheer nylon instead of the drab cotton she had worn that morning. But the most startling change was from the neck up.

Expertly-applied makeup had brought out the delicate lines of her face, and a splash of red lipstick made a flame of her full-lipped mouth. Her upswept hair and the harlequin glasses added the final touch.

I breathed, "Why, you're beautiful!"

She clasped her hands and laughed as delightedly as a child.

I hadn't seen the revolving door rotate a second time. My eyes had been too busy with Helen. But now at my side Mavis said in a grim voice, "I told her you'd say that when you saw her."

I glanced at Mavis. She wasn't looking at me. She was staring at Helen, and the expression on her face wasn't pleasant.

The four of us had dinner in the hotel restaurant, as usual. Dewey looked astonished for about thirty seconds when he saw the transformation his sister had undergone, but then he seemed to adjust to it and accept it as a matter of course.

I wondered if an atomic attack would wipe the doltish expression off his face for any length of time.

Helen herself was a delightful mixture of glamour girl and child. She was by far the smartest-looking woman in the dining room, but her mannerisms were still those of an unsure youngster on her first date. For one thing, she had difficulty walking on her high heels. For another, she couldn't quite believe her own transformation, and kept gazing surreptitiously at a mirror on the wall which reflected our table.

Evenings, the Croissant dining room had a three-piece orchestra consisting of a piano, drums and a horn man who alternated between a saxophone, clarinet and trumpet. The tables were arranged so as to leave a small space for dancing, and I asked Helen if she would like to dance.

She looked at me and said in a stricken voice, as though she thought I would immediately call off our wedding plans, "I don't know how."

It struck me as so funny that the most beautiful woman in the room had so successfully concealed her beauty for thirty-two years that she'd never even been on a dance floor, I laughed aloud. Helen looked so woebegone I had to apologize.

"I'll teach you after we're settled in Westfield," I assured her.

Though Helen was two years older than Mavis, she gave the impression of being much younger. Not just younger than the prim, spinsterish woman Mavis was now, but even younger than Mavis was when dressed in feminine clothes and practicing all the tricks she knew. This wasn't a matter of physical appearance so much as a difference in manner. Mavis, as her real self, left no doubt in any man's mind that she was a mature, experienced woman of the world. Helen possessed the intriguing freshness of a teen-ager.

It occurred to me that it had been the similar quality of youthful innocence which had first attracted me to Mavis years back.

We didn't do anything after dinner because of the full day ahead of us on Sunday. When we parted in the upper hall to go to our separate rooms, Helen whispered to me in a tone of confidence, "You know, Sam, I have a wonderful feeling that with you I'm finally going to begin to live."

I thought wryly that it would have been more accurate if she had said she was finally going to begin to die.

The thought stuck with me long after I got to bed, and for some reason it made me restless. It couldn't have been conscience, for I killed whatever conscience I had years ago. It just seemed a shame to have to destroy so much beauty after bringing it to life.

None of the others had been able to attain more than passable looks, even under Mavis's expert tutelage. And some had verged on the edge of ugliness.

We were married at four o'clock Sunday afternoon, with Dewey and Mavis standing up for us. In her white knit suit Helen made a lovely bride. The J.P.'s wife cried a little.

Afterward, we had a mild celebration in the hotel cocktail lounge, then dinner as usual. It was only eight o'clock when we left the restaurant.

In the lobby Mavis announced somewhat coolly that she was going to bed early and went upstairs. After a moment Dewey seemed to get the idea too, and went off also, leaving Helen and me alone.

Helen gazed at me in sudden panic.

Giving her a reassuring smile, I went over to the desk and had a few moments' conversation with the clerk.

When I rejoined her, Helen asked fearfully, "What were you doing?"

"Canceling your room," I said easily. "I registered you in mine."

When she gazed at me wide-eyed, I said, "I explained to the clerk that we'd just been married. Don't look so alarmed. It's all quite legal."

She gave me a tentative smile. "I'm not scared," she said bravely.

With Mavis as a standard, the most repugnant part of my past lonely-heart marriages had always been the wedding night, for the women were invariably either fat or bony, and dreadfully inhibited on top of it.

Helen was as beautifully proportioned as a Greek statue, and while she was rather becomingly frightened at first, her inhibitions melted with astonishing speed. Once she was able to relax, I discovered a fiery passion in her which amazed me.

For the first time in the five years we had been married, I found myself comparing one of my temporary wives to Mavis and relegating Mavis to second place.

Another thing that surprised me, though it hardly disturbed me, was that Helen wasn't a virgin. Few of my wives ever had been, which had often led me to the reflection that even the plainest woman is unlikely to escape at least some sex experience if she lives long enough. But it did surprise me in Helen's case because of the isolated farm life she had lived. I wondered what drifting farm hand or itinerant drummer had been the lucky man, and what

136

momentary dreams he had brought into her drab life at the time. Dreams which inevitably must have faded to the wry realization that she had served only as a temporary relief from boredom when the man moved on and she never heard from him again.

CHAPTER XVI

EARLY MONDAY morning we checked out of the hotel and started the long drive to Westfield, New York. I figured the total distance at nine hundred and twenty miles, and planned to make it in two days, stopping over approximately halfway at Indianapolis. Mavis and I had to alternate on all the driving, as both Dewey and Helen said they couldn't drive.

Tuesday morning I sent a wire from Indianapolis to Herman Gwynn telling him that we'd arrive some time that evening. We reached Westfield about seven P.M. and had dinner in a restaurant on Main Street. I asked our waiter to recommend a hotel and he told us to try the Greystone a block up the street.

I suspected this was the only hotel in town, but nevertheless it proved an excellent suggestion. It wasn't very modern, but it possessed a wonderfully homey small-town atmosphere, and the rooms were immaculate.

After we were settled, I phoned Herman Gwynn at his home, told him we'd arrived safely, and made an appointment to see him at the store at nine in the morning.

I took Helen along with me the next morning. In the past I had always kept my temporary wives in the background as much as possible in order to discourage possible speculation as to why a man of my pleasing if not handsome appearance and my apparent sound common

138

sense had ever taken such a colorless spouse. But I didn't have to hide Helen. I found myself actually wanting to show her off.

Mavis had picked three dresses for her, plus accessories, including three pairs of shoes. Today she wore a plain blue wool dress a trifle more conservative than the white knit one, but still one that didn't hide her figure. Neat suede pumps with lower heels than the shoes of her wedding outfit created a smart effect without making her wobble as though she were on stilts. A blue cloth coat and a cute little felt hat completed the outfit.

Mavis knew how to shop for clothes, and Helen's transformed appearance bore little resemblance to the cost of the clothing. Mavis had picked items more for style than lasting quality, on the assumption that they wouldn't be in use for more than a few weeks. The total outlay for Helen's entire trousseau had only been about a hundred and fifty dollars.

But on Helen they looked like Saks' Fifth Avenue.

Herman Gwynn proved to be a plump, friendly man nearing seventy. He was obviously impressed by both Helen and me, in that order.

"Glad to meet both of you, Mr. and Mrs. Howard," he said, pumping my hand and grinning with open admiration at Helen. "Your husband warned me he might bring along a new bride, and now I've met you, I can see why he wasn't sure. Must have had to pry you away from a dozen other suitors."

Helen blushed prettily at the compliment, but she didn't look as totally at a loss as she would have a few days before. Already she was beginning to get used to being beautiful.

"I had to get her drunk and marry her before she sobered up," I told the old man.

Gwynn chuckled. "I hope you'll both be as happy as my wife and I have been for near on to fifty years of married life. If we arrange a deal, maybe you'll be happy in the same place."

He took us around the store then. It wasn't a large place, having about a thirty-foot front and a fifty-foot depth. It was arranged much like the average hardware store, except that a good many of the items offered for sale were heavier equipment than would ordinarily be found in a hardware store. In the case of large items such as cream separators, there was only one of each in stock. Gwynn explained that he kept them as display models only, and ordered each time a sale was made.

The sales clerk was a brisk young man in his early twenties named Harold Manning. Gwynn explained that he was relatively new and was looking around for some job with more future, so that his possible layoff wouldn't be much of a handicap to him. The female bookkeeper presented more of a problem, however, he said. She was a middle-aged spinster named Ida Kroll, and had been an employee of the store for fifteen years.

When I told him I planned to replace her with Helen in the event we took over the store, he said, "Well, she ought to be able to get another job easy enough. I'd give her a top reference. Don't let her influence your figuring."

After we finished our initial inspection of the place, I asked, "How big a hurry are you in to dispose of this business, Mr. Gwynn?"

He rubbed his plump chin. "Well, I dunno. Sooner I get rid of it, the sooner I can move my wife to a warmer climate. She's got neuritis so bad, she's had to spend most of the winter on her back the last couple of years. Just what you mean?"

"We're both pretty enthusiastic about the setup," I explained. "Even more so, now that we've seen the place and got a glimpse of the town. But we're utter strangers in these parts, and we want a chance to see how we like the town itself before we jump into a business which is going to tie us here permanently. What I had in mind was to rent a house here and take our time looking over the business and the town before we made the final move."

"How long a time?" he asked dubiously.

"Say six weeks. Meantime I'd make all arrangements with the bank, so that as soon as papers are signed you could get your full purchase price. Matter of fact, I was going to ask you to step over to the bank with me now and settle that part."

"Oh, I wouldn't object to your taking that long," Gwynn said, brightening. "With the Christmas holidays coming up, we wouldn't move that soon anyway. Sure, I'll be glad to introduce you at the bank."

At the Westfield branch of the Chautauqua National Bank and Trust Company of Jamestown, things went as smoothly as I expected. When we went in to talk to the manager, I let my exhibits do most of my talking for me.

The branch manager was a quiet-spoken man of middle age named Bradford Crane. First I handed him my bank draft for seven thousand dollars and Helen's for eight thousand, explaining that we wanted to open a joint savings account for ten thousand and a joint checking account for the balance. Then I showed him my copy of my letter to the Westfield Chamber of Commerce and the Chamber's reply. And finally I placed on his desk the neatly forged character and credit references vouching for my honesty and my varied experience in retail merchandising.

I wasn't worried about any of the references being checked. When a man starts talking business by opening accounts totaling fifteen thousand dollars, even a conservative banker isn't likely to be suspicious of him. Particularly when the loan he asks for is on a local business with which he can't possibly abscond, and the bank would be fully protected by the mortgage even if the borrower defaulted.

Bradford Crane didn't even hesitate. When he had finished studying my array of documents, he said, "I don't think you'll have to worry about backing if you decide to take over the store, Mr. Howard. This bank will be glad to do business with you."

That completed the first phase of my plan by establishing in Herman Gwynn's mind that I not only meant business, but was financially capable of swinging the deal. And it hadn't cost me a thing.

It never would, of course. After the funeral everybody concerned would as usual be too sympathetic to show more than mild disappointment when I backed out of everything and left town to escape sorrowful memories.

The rest of that day Helen, Dewey, Mavis and I all spent house hunting. Herman Gwynn got on the phone, and through his contacts with the Westfield Businessmen's Club, of which he was a member, managed to locate two houses for us to look at. As nearly as he could discover, they were the only two in town for rent.

The first one was one side of a duplex, and when we learned that it wasn't going to be vacant until after the first of the year, we went away without even looking at it. The second was a two-story furnished place on Portage Street, within easy walking distance of the store, and available immediately. It was only available until March, however, as the owners were wintering in Florida and wanted it vacated for their own use when they returned to town.

The downstairs consisted of four rooms: living room, dining room, kitchen and a bedroom. Upstairs there were two bedrooms plus a wide hall. An open stairway led upstairs from the front room, and at its top only a balustrade guarded the front side of the upper hall. I examined the twelve-foot drop from the balustrade to the front-room floor thoughtfully as we went up the stairs.

Catching me studying it, Mavis gave me a sardonic smile.

Then Dewey did something helpful for a change. Resting his hand on the railing as he reached the top of the stairs, he said, "Hey, this thing's kind of loose."

He shook it in demonstration, and sure enough it moved back and forth shakily.

"I better have that fixed," the agent said.

I walked over to where the railing joined the wall, noting that the nails in the end posts had begun to work loose.

"Don't bother," I said. "I can fix that myself easily."

I wouldn't, of course. And I was reasonably certain Dewey would never think of it again, unless he happened to fall through it and spoil it for subsequent use. But it was convenient to have planted in the real estate agent's mind that the thing was in a dangerous condition.

We all agreed that the place was ideal for our purposes, and I paid the agent a month's rent in advance. We moved from the hotel to the house that evening. Helen and I took one of the upstairs bedrooms, Mavis took the other, and we relegated Dewey to the one on the first floor.

The next day was Thanksgiving, and we spent it at home except for a noon meal in a restaurant. We had to eat out because the women hadn't had time to shop and the stores weren't open on Thanksgiving Day.

On Friday I began my study of the farm appliance business while the two women did the necessary shopping and organizing attendant to setting up housekeeping. I spent the entire day with Herman Gwynn and his two clerks, going over the books for several years past, making a detailed examination of the stock and listening to the three of them explain the details of the business.

During the next few weeks our lives settled into pretty much of a pattern. I spent a good deal of time studying the business, meeting other local businessmen and generally getting acquainted with the community. One of the businessmen I particularly cultivated was an insurance agent named Richard Slack.

I never mentioned the subject of insurance to him, however, leaving it to him to bring it up at the proper time, as I knew he would. But I did arrange for the proper time. I invited him to dinner.

No insurance man ever deliberately sidesteps a possible sale. After dinner when we were all seated in the front room and I dropped the remark that I didn't have any life insurance on myself, Slack went to work at once.

"Now that you're married, you certainly ought to have some protection for your wife, Mr. Howard," he said. "Not that I'm trying to sell you a policy. I don't believe

144

in taking advantage of people's hospitality to talk business. But as a matter of principle I'm naturally a strong believer in insurance."

Despite his avowed reluctance to take advantage of our hospitality, it didn't take much urging for him to go out to his car and bring in his brief case. Within an hour of the time we had gotten up from dinner he had me signed up for a ten-thousand-dollar straight life policy.

Then he suggested, "How about your wife, Mr. Howard. Has she any insurance?"

Chuckling, I told him I wasn't interested in betting on my wife's death.

"That's not the way to look at insurance," he said seriously. "It's not a gamble. It's an investment. She ought to have at least enough to cover funeral expenses."

He went to work on both me and Helen then, and ended up selling me a five-thousand-dollar policy on her life, to go in force in thirty days. After that he made a stab at selling policies to Mavis and Dewey without getting anywhere with either. Mavis told him she had a five-hundred-dollar policy to cover her funeral expenses and wasn't interested in any more, and Dewey didn't even seem to know what he was talking about. Finally he gave up on both of them.

I was satisfied with the whole evening. When it came time for the insurance company to pay off, there wasn't likely to be much suspicion when the agent recalled that he had considerable difficulty convincing me my wife should be insured as well as myself, and instead of insuring her for the largest amount I could get, he had trouble getting me up to a five-thousand-dollar policy.

CHAPTER XVII

WHILE I busied myself with studying the farm appliance business and getting acquainted with the community, Mavis spent enough time ostensibly looking for a job to create the impression that she really wanted one, though she would have been considerably put out if anyone had actually offered her a position. Dewey seemed content to loll around the house waiting for the expected opening at the store to develop.

Helen threw herself wholeheartedly into housekeeping duties.

We discovered that Westfield was a charming village. There were many lovely old homes, and most streets were lined with ancient elms. At the moment these were bare, but it wasn't hard to visualize that when the winter passed, the streets would be beautiful green-roofed arcades. While it was an old town, there seemed to be some money in it, for most of the large old frame buildings were well kept up.

Mixed with the old-fashioned element which made the town so comfortable was a good deal of modernism, too. The stores of the shopping center were as streamlined as any in large cities, there was an excellent first-run movie theater, and even one or two glittering cocktail lounges. The net effect was of a wealth of tradition, which still reached over into modern times to give the town its pleasant flavor, without the natives al-

146

lowing it to sap their vitality. For despite its quietly homey atmosphere, I sensed a good deal of vitality and forward thinking among Westfield's businessmen.

It wasn't hard to fall in love with the town.

My relationship with Helen developed very pleasantly, too. She was an excellent housewife. As we grew to know each other better she developed into a more and more vivacious companion, and she seemed to be pouring out to me all the passionate love which had been bottled up within her for thirty-two years.

Sometimes, in my enjoyment of our day-to-day life, I would forget the eventual plans Mavis and I had for Helen and Dewey to the extent that I would find myself seriously looking forward to the moment when we would take over the Farmer's Appliance Store and become permanent members of the community. Then it was like a dash of cold water in the face when I jerked myself back to reality.

As Christmas neared, Mavis began to grow a little impatient as to when I intended to act. One afternoon while Helen was shopping and Dewey, for a change, was out of the house too, we nearly had a fight.

"Hasn't the insurance been in force long enough?" Mavis demanded.

"Only three weeks," I said. "We'll wait until after the first of the year."

"You mean you expect to spend Christmas as that woman's husband?"

"I certainly don't expect to spend it in mourning," I snapped at her. "What's the matter with you?"

"Nothing with me," she said. "I'm beginning to wonder what's the matter with you."

I discovered what was the matter with me Christmas

Eve. We had a tree with the usual exchange of presents, and Helen acted as delighted as a child. She had given me a new robe and slippers. My gift to her, which made Mavis stare at me balefully, was a tiny gold wristwatch for which I had paid the unnecessary price of seventy-five dollars.

I had given Mavis a scarf and a pair of gloves.

In bed that night Helen was still showering me with excited thanks for the watch. And as she whispered into my ear, I suddenly realized something I must have known subconsciously for some time.

I was in love with Helen.

As I lay there with Helen in my arms, thinking about my new discovery, I realized not only that I was in love with her, but that it was the first time in my life I had ever been really in love. Whatever it was I had felt for Mavis, it had no comparison to this overwhelming desire to protect and live the rest of my life with the soft creature lying next to me.

All at once, I knew with great certainty that all Mavis's and my plans were off. I intended to take over Gwynn's store, I intended to make it pay, and I intended to live in this town with Helen as my wife permanently.

The decision involved considerable alternate planning. I knew it was no use trying to explain it to Mavis, for she would never accept a simple ultimatum to get out of my life and stay out. I remembered a scene a year or two back when Mavis had suspected I was carrying on a flirtation with a blonde during one of our periodic vacations. It was one of the few times I ever saw her really angry, and the only time she ever dared talk to me in the tone she used that night.

She had said, "I've let you push me around since the

day we met, Sam. I've done everything you told me. I've let you make a killer out of me. I've watched you live with other women, burning with jealousy, even though I knew they meant nothing to you. I would have let you push me into bed with other men, if you'd wanted to run that kind of a racket. There isn't anything in the world I wouldn't do for you. Except one thing. Give you up." Then she had screamed in complete rage, "That blonde's no mark. You stay away from her!"

No, Mavis wouldn't accept my change of plans. I knew that even suggesting it would bring on a tornado which would make her rage over my mild flirtation with the blonde seem like a gentle spring breeze. In all probability she would create a scene which would end with both of us on trial for our lives in a half-dozen different states.

There was really only one solution, I realized.

I was going to have to kill Mavis.

I reached the decision quite calmly. Five years earlier, just the thought of killing Mavis would have appalled me. But I had gotten a lot of practice in murder since then. It had become such a part of my life that it was the logical solution to any problem.

I started my campaign a few days later by telling Mavis in private that I was beginning to miss her so much, I wanted to arrange for us to get away for a few days.

"I don't want to pull this thing until a couple of weeks after New Year's," I said. "When people have had a chance to get over the holidays. Before that we couldn't get a judge to act on unfreezing the bank accounts, and we'd just have to sit and sweat it out anyway. But I'm going crazy for you. I can't wait three more weeks."

Mavis was so overjoyed at the suggestion that it didn't even occur to her this was the first time I had ever violated my strict rule of never dropping our brother-sister relationship, even temporarily, when we were on a job.

"How will we work it?" she asked breathlessly.

"Buffalo's only sixty miles from here. Suppose that right after New Year's you announce you have a job offer in Buffalo and have to go up there to check it. I'll offer to drive you up. We'll leave on Wednesday the sixth and stay over until Friday night."

"Suppose Helen wants to go along?"

"I can handle Helen," I said.

On Monday, January fourth, Mavis began putting the plan in operation. At dinner she announced that she had spotted an ad for a stenographer in the Buffalo *Courier Express,* had phoned the prospective employer long distance, and had an appointment to see him Wednesday afternoon.

"I think I'll stay for a couple of days and see what Buffalo's like while I'm up there," she remarked.

I made no comment at the time. I waited until the following evening at dinner.

Then I said, "A number of Gwynn's suppliers are in Buffalo. I've been thinking of running up to talk to them and get their slant on the store. Think I'll drive Mavis up and spend a couple of days there myself."

Helen voiced no objection whatever, nor did she invite herself along, apparently feeling that I'd be too busy with suppliers to bother with her. Mavis and I left early Wednesday morning.

When we reached Buffalo, I drove straight to J. N.

Adams' instead of registering at a hotel. When I parked in front of the department store, Mavis looked at me puzzledly.

"What are we going to do here?" she asked.

"I'm going down the street and kill some time in the first tavern I see," I said. "You're going into J. N. Adams' and get an outfit that makes you look like a woman instead of an old-maid school teacher." I handed her five twenty-dollar bills. "Don't go overboard, because you're only buying these clothes to wear for a couple of days, but if we're going to have a short second honeymoon, I want you to look the part."

I told her I'd give her an hour and meet her back at the car.

Promptly at the end of an hour I found her waiting at the car with a happy expression on her face and two suit boxes under her arm.

"Spend it all?" I asked.

"Hardly half of it," she said. "But wait till you see what I got."

She was so eager to get back into something feminine, she insisted on going straight to a hotel before we even had lunch. I registered us at the Richford as Mr. and Mrs. Sam Parker of Brooklyn.

As soon as the bellhop left us alone, Mavis disappeared into the bathroom with her two boxes. She was gone nearly twenty minutes, and when she came out again she was a different woman.

She wore a white quilted skirt of heavy satin, so tight across the hips that their firm roundness was brought out in sharp relief, and an ebony black blouse open at the throat, with the V dipping to the shadowed cleft between her breasts. She had loosened her hair from

151

its old-maidish bun and had brushed it to fall loosely about her shoulders. Expertly-applied makeup completed her transformation.

"You did all that on fifty bucks?" I asked admiringly.

"Plus a clearance-sale coat for only nineteen dollars."

Going back into the bathroom, she returned wearing the new coat. It was of gray cloth and tailored as simply as the one she wore with her spinsterish suits. But instead of being severe, its lines somehow managed to create an effect of complete femininity.

"Can you appear in public with me now without feeling ashamed?" she asked.

"I'll have to fight off the wolves," I told her.

CHAPTER XVIII

We decided to keep to restaurants off the beaten track and to the lesser-known night clubs while we were in Buffalo in order to decrease the risk of unexpectedly running into someone who knew us in Westfield. In a city the size of Buffalo, there wasn't much chance of this happening, but on the other hand, Westfield residents often drove the sixty miles to shop there. Mavis, herself, understood that it would be difficult to explain her changed appearance if we did run into anyone we knew, and made no objection to keeping our celebration rather furtive.

That night when we went to bed, Mavis brought out another item she had purchased—a nightgown. Its purpose was obviously entirely decorative, for it was much too sheer to have any warmth to it.

I didn't go to sleep when Mavis did. I deliberately lay awake for another hour, then carefully eased out of bed. When I was sure my movement hadn't awakened her, I quietly collected all of her new clothes in the dark and carried them into the bathroom. I eased the door shut behind me before turning on the bathroom light.

With a razor blade I removed every label from her clothes, even the small tab sewed into the seam of her slip. Then I turned out the light again and quietly returned each item to where it had been.

As I slipped back into bed, Mavis stirred and said sleepily, "What's the matter, honey?"

"Nothing," I said, drawing her into my arms. "Just go back to sleep."

At dinner the next night, I suggested we do what many other honeymooners do and take a run up to Niagara Falls that evening.

"At this time of year?" she asked. "Don't the falls freeze in winter?"

"Sure," I said. "But they're supposed to be even more beautiful frozen than running. It's only twenty-two miles."

"Wouldn't it be pretty late when we got there?"

"At night's when you're supposed to see them," I explained. "They play colored lights on them from the Canadian side."

"All right," she said agreeably.

I hadn't made the suggestion until eight o'clock. By the time we finished dinner, got back to the hotel, packed and checked out, it was nine-thirty. I told Mavis we were checking out because we'd stay over in Niagara Falls that night.

I took my time making the trip. It was a clear night, cold but without snow, and it was comfortable enough driving with the heater on. It was just ten-fifteen when we reached the city of Niagara Falls.

"Will we spend the night over in Canada?" Mavis asked. "I understand the Canadian side is where most of the tourists go."

"If you'd like. I thought we'd stop long enough to take a look at the falls from this side, then go over the bridge and see how they look from Canada."

Actually I had no intention of crossing International Bridge. I knew the immigration service lifted car registrations at the bridge and returned them when visitors came back over it. Whether they kept track of the number of people in each car, I had no idea, but I wasn't going to chance having to explain on the way back why my passenger had stayed in Canada.

I didn't have any difficulty finding my way around, as the main routes of the town were dotted with directional signs. A little after ten-thirty we reached the park on the American side of the falls.

"Oh, look!" Mavis said. "The lights across the river are on!"

It was a magnificent sight. For a thousand feet, a frozen curtain of ice some hundred and sixty feet high stretched to Goat Island. And beyond the island, for another two thousand feet, the Horseshoe Falls reached toward the Canadian shore. Two dozen huge searchlights at Queen Victoria Park bathed the glittering ice in constantly-changing colors.

As I had expected, there weren't many people outdoors on so cold a night, even with such a beautiful spectacle to watch. The parking lights of one or two other cars could be seen in the park, but I had deliberately stopped some distance from any of them. There were no pedestrians at all in sight.

"Let's get out a minute," I suggested.

Obediently, Mavis climbed out of the car and followed me over to the observation rail, huddling so close to me because of the unexpectedly cutting wind, we probably looked like a single person from a distance. I hoped that the people in the other cars were far enough off so that they couldn't see us at all. But even if they could, I doubted that they would be able to make out whether

155

we were one or two persons. And certainly they couldn't distinguish what we were doing.

At the observation railing there was not even the protection of trees to break the steady force of the wind. When I put my arm about Mavis, she shivered even in its protection. Neither of us said anything, momentarily held spellbound by the gigantic spectacle. Conversation would have been difficult anyway because of the combined roar of falling water and the wind.

Beneath the ice I realized that water was tumbling down as usual. Below us, in a gorge between perpendicular walls two hundred and fifty feet high, there were gaps of open water in the frozen lower river. In the summertime the whole stretch would be boiling rapids, I realized, but it was frozen to relative sluggishness now.

Somewhere beyond the rapids, I knew, lay the famous whirlpool.

Glancing around, I could see no cars other than the ones which had been there when we arrived. And even as I looked, the nearest one flicked on its lights and drove away.

Gently I took Mavis's purse from her hand.

"What do you want?" she shouted up into my face over the combined roar of water and wind.

"Your identification," I said in a normal tone she couldn't possibly have heard.

Looping the strap of the purse over my wrist, I spun her around, grasped her under both arms and heaved her over the railing.

She probably screamed, but I couldn't hear it over the sound of the falls and the whistling wind.

I removed her wallet from the purse, checked over the other items to make sure there was nothing in it to identify the body as that of Mavis Howard, and tossed the purse after her.

With bad luck, I figured, her body would be discovered the next day. With good luck, if it got under the ice, not until Spring. And in either event, it would neither be identified nor conform to the description of anyone reported missing. It was hardly likely that anyone reading the description of the dead woman's extremely feminine clothing would ever associate her with the plainly-dressed Mavis.

The simple explanation that my sister had taken the stenographic job she had gone to Buffalo to see about, had to start work immediately and had asked me to forward her clothes would serve as a temporary excuse for her absence from Westfield. Eventually I could receive word that she was moving back to Florida.

I contemplated disposing of her weekend bag, which now had in it the suit she was wearing when we left Westfield. Then I decided it would be safer to smuggle it back into the house and pack it right in with everything else when I ostensibly got ready to ship her clothes to Buffalo.

I stayed in a tourist cabin just outside of Buffalo that night. I went to sleep dreaming of Helen.

Helen and Dewey weren't expecting Mavis and me back until late Friday night, but there was now no reason to waste all of Friday. I was up at six A.M. and on the road by six-thirty. At eight in the morning I pulled into our garage.

I came in the back door quietly, as Dewey usually slept late and I didn't want to disturb him. The door to his room was open, but he wasn't in it and the bed was made. I was a little surprised, as I'd never seen him up this early before, and certainly had never before known him to make his own bed.

My feet made no sound on the carpeted steps as I went upstairs. At the top, I grinned at the loose balustrade, resolving to fix it that morning as soon as I had kissed Helen hello.

Apparently Helen was still asleep, as the door to our bedroom was closed. Quietly I went into Mavis's room, hung her coat in the closet, unpacked her bag and put the items away. I put the bag at the back of the closet.

Then I was turning the knob of Helen's and my bedroom. I pushed the door open gently, smiling a little in anticipation of seeing her soft blonde hair spread across the pillow.

The smile froze. Helen was in bed all right, but her arm was thrown in sleep across the bare chest of Dewey and her head was nestled on his shoulder.

I was just standing there in stupefied shock when Dewey's eyes suddenly popped open. For a long moment we stared at each other, neither speaking. Then he abruptly sat erect, pushing Helen unceremoniously to one side, and his hand darted under his pillow.

An instant later I was staring into the bore of a .45 automatic.

"Come in, Mr. Howard," Dewey said. The stupid expression was gone from his face and his voice was crisp. Suddenly he looked older than the twenty-two years he was supposed to be. His gangling awkwardness and doltish expression had merely created the illusion of youth. With sick astonishment I realized he was a fully mature man, possibly as old as Helen.

His lips spread in a tight smile as he swung his legs

over the side of the bed and came erect. He was wearing only pajama bottoms.

Helen had sat erect, the covers falling to her waist to reveal she had been sleeping nude. Her full lips thinned to a narrow line.

"Where's Mavis?" she asked sharply.

I let out a humorless laugh. "She stayed in Buffalo."

"Permanently? You mean she took the job?"

"Permanently," I said dryly.

Dewey commanded, "Turn around and lean against the wall. With your hands flat on it."

I stared at him until his lips thinned and his finger across the trigger began to tense. Then I turned my back and placed both hands against the wall. A moment later the gun muzzle dug into my spine and quick but efficient hands moved over me.

"Okay," Dewey said. "Turn around again."

When I turned, I discovered that Helen had slipped into a robe.

"This isn't incest, is it?" I said to her.

Staring at me, she emitted a sharp little laugh. "Incest? Dewey's my husband, you damned fool." She looked at Dewey. "We'll have to do it now. We can take care of Mavis later, but we'll have to do this now."

Dewey motioned toward the only straight-backed chair in the room. "Take your choice," he offered. "Sit or catch a bullet in the guts."

I decided to sit in the chair.

With a couple of neckties from the tie rack in my closet Helen expertly tied my hands and feet while Dewey held me under his gun. Then she effectively gagged me with a couple of handkerchiefs from my dresser drawer.

159

Dewey went out of the room. In the hall I could hear the reluctant screech of nails tearing loose as he pushed the upper hall railing forward. After a few moments there was a rending sound and then the crash of lumber falling into the front room.

Dewey came back and looked at me. "Suppose the first drop doesn't kill him?" he asked.

"Then we'll carry him up and drop him again," Helen said calmly.

She stooped to loosen the necktie binding my ankles enough so that I could walk at a hobbling gait.

"Get on your feet, my love," she said. "You're going to take a short walk."

www.ingramcontent.com/pod-product-compliance
Lightning Source LLC
Chambersburg PA
CBHW031127210626
46816CB00015B/1148